COMING H

A SWEETBRIAR BAY NOVEL

Book One

BY

PIPER REECE

This is work of fiction. All of the names, characters, organizations, places and events and incidents are used fictitiously or products of the author's imagination.

Edited By Karen Hrdlicka

You can also find Piper, who has a sexier alter ego named Ty Langston at (**http://www.tylangston.com**/)

For exclusive content and for the most up to date news, sign up to be a part of The Pied Pipers here.[1]

---

1. https://www.facebook.com/groups/344054220499983

For Mom and Gert – xoxo

Chapter 1

"Kat? Kat, where are you?" a male voice shouted through a bustling newsroom. His British accent was firm as it filtered through the sounds of typing fingers, printers, and others talking on the phone.

The man began to move around the maze of the room. He was a short, middle-aged man with a receding hairline with silver temples. His gray eyes twinkled with excitement when he decided to stop at the copy editors' group of desks at the far end corner of the room.

Out of breath, he asked. "Any of you see Kat McKinnon?"

The small group of copy editors never looked up from what they were doing on their computers. They clicked their mouses and stared at the screens, trying to make sure that their stories made deadline.

"No," one replied. "We haven't seen her."

"Crap!" the man yelled while he leaned against one of the cubicles. "That interview she wanted is on the phone!"

"What interview?" said a young woman, who was walking up the hallway with a blue box in one hand while eating a chocolate éclair in the other.

The man's eyebrows lifted. He smiled. "There you are! I have been looking all over for you," he told her.

"Hey, Ross! I went to Sweet Dreams Bakery and got everyone some donuts and éclairs. Who needs a sugar rush?" she asked everyone with a huge smile.

Suddenly, the taps and clicks turned into cheers and clapping. The British man's lips softened into a smile at the young woman.

Everyone gazed with cheerful glee at Katherine McKinnon. Her warm and funny personality always set a positive tone at the *Empire Post*.

As one of the hottest lifestyle personalities in the country, "Kat" as her friends called her was constantly watched not only for her journalism skills, but also her trendy wardrobe. On this late summer day, her slender frame wore a cute sleeveless, belted, blue chambray dress. Her dark purple manicured hand placed the blue bakery box down carefully on an empty desk across from the copy editors.

Her sunglasses were perched on top of her mass of long, brown beach waves. Her brown eyes turned toward her boss, Ross, who was now next to her. The two of them began to walk through the newsroom.

"You got him!" he replied.

Her lips pursed and eyes narrowed. "Got who?" she asked while placing another bite of the éclair in her mouth.

"Jacques Primeau!" her editor said with glee.

Her eyes narrowed as she continued to chew her éclair. She could not believe what she was hearing. Jacques Primeau was only one of the best chef's and television personalities in the country.

Her nude lips curved slowly into a smile. "The Jacques Primeau?" she asked

Ross nodded. "Yep. He's apparently a huge fan of yours! His assistant will be calling you later to set up the interview."

Kat jumped up and down with happiness. She had been at the *Empire Post* since she graduated college. She worked her way up from being editorial assistant to one of the most popular lifestyle writers in the country. She was getting so popular that she was now being courted by TV networks, begging her to do regular lifestyle spots on beauty, fashion, food, style, and the occasional celebrity interview.

Her childhood was flooded with memories of her father watching Jacques Primeau every Friday night, while trying to replicate the show's main dishes for her mother and sisters for dinner.

Another career highlight she could check off her list.

Not bad for a girl who used to live in a town with the population of 10,000. In her small town of Sweetbriar, Georgia, she would dream about writing articles and books on the latest and greatest things people were doing. From gardening to wearing the perfect flat. She wanted to be one of the first women of color who could gauge the gaudy to the trendy.

Forgetting that she had the éclair in her hand, Kat threw her hands around her boss. Ross yelped when he heard and felt the éclair slam against the back of his shirt.

"Holy shit, Ross! I did it!" she squealed. "I can't believe it! This means so much to me!" She pulled away and looked in horror at the remnants of éclair on Ross's shoulder. "Your shirt! I'm so sorry."

The editor-in-chief snickered. He took her chocolate and custard filled hand in his and replied, "It's fine, dear. Nothing a little trip to the cleaners can't fix."

Kat nodded. "Which cleaners?"

"Henderson's on 9th. A little extra starch please. Helps keep the wrinkles out."

"Least I can do. When I was a kid, my dad and I used to watch Jacques Primeau on television every single Friday night. My mom wasn't the greatest cook growing up. That talent went to my father and grandmother. I learned to make everything from how to make a cheese soufflé to spaghetti carbonara from watching his show." Her eyes filled with happy tears as she continued, "From my table to yours..."

Ross and she said together, "Bon Appetite."

Both laughed together as they continued to walk to her desk.

"Kat, we are all so proud of you. You deserve all of this. All the late nights, the traveling, the answering phones, the obits. You worked hard for this moment."

"Thanks, Ross. It means a lot," she said as she went into her cubicle and sat down.

"By the way, someone at WNTV called. I assume they want you to do some sort of lifestyle segment."

Kat nodded as she sifted through the organized chaos of her desk and turned on her computer. "What are you, the receptionist today?" she quipped.

Ross leaned against the side of her cubicle and said, "Don't you realize, dear Katherine, that part of my job is to not only give out assignments to my fine staff, but it's also to fix grammar, hunt all of you down, and answer phone calls so that said fine staff doesn't miss important phone calls from famous people, who bring in readers and then advertisers and accordingly keep us all employed."

Kat turned and looked at him. "Got it."

"Good girl. I'll be in my office, trying to hunt down another star reporter," he told her as he walked away. "By the way, I'll leave my shirt on the desk. You can pick it up when you leave."

Kat laughed. "Yes, sir."

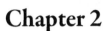

Chapter 2

It was late afternoon and Kat was busy at her cubicle typing away. Her dry, half-eaten éclair was on the corner of her desk. She spent the rest of the afternoon gathering more research for her upcoming interview with Chef Jacques Primeau when her cell phone went off.

"Hello?" she asked as she picked up her phone. Her large brown eyes were filled with concentration while she stared at her computer screen.

"Hey, babe, it's me," a male voice said.

Kat smiled at the voice. She quickly looked around the nearly empty newsroom and placed the phone on speaker.

"Hey there! How was your day?" she asked.

"It was good. Sold the penthouse for The Greenbergs," the male voice stated proudly.

"The Greenbergs?" she asked

"Yes, THE Greenbergs. You know Martin and Christine Greenberg? One of the hottest and richest couples in New York City."

Kat was multi-tasking as usual. She continued to type on her computer when she remembered who The Greenbergs were. "Oh, them," she said mid word. "Isn't Christine Greenberg that popular gallery owner whose husband owns that club everyone is talking about?"

"Yes," he told her. "Her husband owns the Pure Nightclub. She's also a huge fan of yours, by the way. In fact, I promised her that I would introduce you to her if they went through with the sale," he informed her.

"Awe, Mitch. Did you?"

"I did," he said sounding nervous. "Was that, okay?"

"Normally, I'd be happy to. But I got the interview with that chef I was telling you about. Going to be on a time crunch," Kat told him.

"Jacques Primeau?" he asked. "Kat! That's fantastic!"

"Thank you. I'm so excited. You know how long I've wanted to talk to him."

"When's the interview?"

"In a couple of days. He's actually going to be in town. I can't wait to tell my dad. I called Mom earlier and she said for me to surprise him. She was on her way to try a case."

"I'm sure he'll be thrilled. "

"Yeah, I think I'll have Jacques sign one of his first edition books for Daddy as a birthday gift. Watching Jacques was our thing when I was growing up. Mom wasn't the best chef, so every Friday night, Dad and I would watch Jacques' show and cook alongside him." She laughed as she remembered. "Some dishes came out better than others. Those were some fun times."

"Well, between me selling this penthouse and you snagging an interview with your idol, I think we need to celebrate."

"Tonight?" Kat asked

"Yes, tonight," he insisted.

Kat sighed. She was nearly done with her research. All she wanted to do was to go home, take a nice long bath, put some cozy pj's on, and watch some Netflix with some takeout and a glass of wine.

"Can you give me an hour? I'm nearly done here. I have to change and drop off Ross's shirt at the cleaners."

She could hear her boyfriend's snicker on the other end. "Can't your boss do his own dry-cleaning? You're not the help."

"No, I'm not. But I did accidently spill my chocolate éclair all over the back of his shirt. I am more than happy to get it cleaned for him."

"Aah," Mitchell said. "I jumped to conclusions."

"Ross is a good one, honey. In fact, the whole newsroom is. He's a fair guy. Besides, you, my dad, and Jay, he's my biggest cheerleader."

"Jay? "Mitchell asked

She suddenly looked at the phone.

"Jay?" she asked

"You said Jay." he told her.

She couldn't believe she did that. It had been years. The last time she saw him was at a film premiere, years ago. He had some blonde on his arm, and he could have cared less if she were in the same place. Good riddance.

"Jay once did. So, I thought. I haven't thought about him in years. Wonder what brought that on?" she said.

"Good to hear. He seemed like an ass from what you told me. Anyway, I'll meet you at Marino's in an hour. Love you."

"See you soon. Love you too," she replied and promptly ended the call.

Kat glanced at her computer screen once more. She pressed save on her notes and emailed herself the notes to her personal email, just in case she decided to work on her feature after dinner. She looked over at the photo of her and Mitchell and gave it a blank stare.

The night the photo was taken was a happy one. It was some film premiere with an up-and-coming film director that she had just interviewed. She and Mitchell had just begun dating. He had just joined his real estate company at the time and was already one of the top real estate agents in the city. They were happy, newly in love, and on everyone's guest lists.

Her ex-boyfriend, Jayson McQuayde, was also there that night. She hadn't seen him since she left home for college years ago. He was now an NHL star with millions in the bank and a different starlet on his arm every week. His matinee idol looks and Southern charm could make the smartest girl weak in the knees. She should know. It happened to her. She now hated him. So much that she couldn't bear to look at him that night. Not after what he did to her. She deserved better. She got better, she did better.

Fast forward to today. She had the guy. Not only were she and Mitchell still on everyone's guest lists in the city, but now in the country. Mitchell was one of the best real estate agents in the country. She was one of the hottest lifestyle personalities. The grind seemed nonstop at times. Her solace was writing, and any Shonda Rhimes show. Mitchell was the opposite. He loved the nightlife. For him, they were future contacts to a potential sale or a way to move up. He didn't have a lot when she first met him. But he worked hard. He was a proud and good-looking guy with café au lait skin and green eyes. His hair was in a sandy brown buzz cut. Money and status were everything to him. His hard work brought him from the mailroom to the penthouse they shared. He got his family out of the projects into the Upper East Side. As loving as he could be, the chip on his shoulder and thinking the world was against him could bring out the worst, like his thoughts on Ross. She didn't know where that came from. But it disappeared as quickly as it started so she was going to chalk it up to it being him jumping to conclusions. She looked at her phone. Her mom and sister must have called five or six times. It was probably about her snagging the interview, she thought. She'd talk to them later. She stood up, grabbed her phone, jacket, Ross's shirt, and purse and left. Maybe all she needed was a great meal and a laugh with her guy.

Chapter 3

By the time Kat arrived at Marino's, Mitchell was sitting at the table there waiting for her. She was running late. Traffic was backed up due to an accident on this rainy night.

She looked beautiful in a light purple dress with spaghetti straps and a dark purple blazer.

"Hi, reservation for Simmons?" she asked the hostess as she put her umbrella away.

The blonde restaurant hostess looked up and took Kat over to the table. "Here you are, Ms. McKinnon." Kat looked at the woman with surprise. The young hostess smiled and whispered, "I'm sorry. I'm a huge fan of yours. I recognized you the minute you walked in. I hope you don't mind." Kat smiled. She forgot that at times people saw her on television or on YouTube regularly.

"Oh, no problem. Thank you," she told the woman.

Mitchell sat there with a smile on his face while putting down his wine glass.

"Started without me, I see." Kat said to him as she took off her coat and placed her purse down on the table.

"Hope you don't mind. I ordered us a bottle of Dom for the night."

"Well now!" she said as she sat down." "Dom Perignon? This is a happy day."

"Well, both of us got some great news. A splurge every now and then won't hurt."

"Not at all," she agreed.

"The Greenberg's penthouse sold for six million dollars and before you got here, it looks like I may have two more people under contract."

Kat's eyes widened with surprise. "Damn, go you. I'm sorry I was late. I hung up with you and dropped off Ross's shirt at the cleaners and went home and changed. The traffic is crazy tonight," she said.

Mitchell looked at his phone. He began to text.

Kat's stomach began to growl. She looked at the menu. Despite her feeling hungry, there wasn't anything on the menu she really wanted. "Hmm."

"What's up?" Mitchell asked, looking briefly from his phone.

"Can't decide on what I want. I must admit, babe. I'm really not in the mood for Italian this evening," she told him.

"Well, we can always go somewhere else. That sushi place you like is open, as is Fernando's."

"Nah, it's okay. I'm just in research mode with the whole Jacques Primeau story."

"Well, how much research can you do on him? You pretty much know all there is to know about him, Kat," Mitchell said, as he looked at his phone once again and put it down.

"To tell you the truth. I don't. Despite him being on television and his books, he doesn't offer a lot of opportunities for people to discuss his personal life. I'll definitely discuss his upbringing and his training, but sometimes people just want a taste of what makes the person who they are."

"Got it," he said.

A waitress suddenly came up to the table. She was short and petite with her long brown hair in a neat ponytail. She looked as if she had been working for hours. Her blue eyes were ringed with dark circles. "Hi there." she greeted. "My name is Heather. I'm your waitress for the evening. Can I get you anything?"

Mitchell glanced at the woman with barely an acknowledgement. "Yes, we'll both have the eggplant parmesan, some calamari, and can I have another glass for the lady, please?" he asked.

Kat looked at the woman and smiled. Mitchell's tone toward the woman seemed cold.

"No problem, sir," said the waitress as she grabbed the menus. "I'll be back with your order," she told them and walked away.

Kat looked over at Mitchell as he continued to look and text on his phone. Mitchell looked up at Kat.

"What?" he asked

"What was that?" Kat questioned.

"What was what?"

"Since when do you order for me?" she asked

"Well, you said you weren't up to it and didn't want to go anywhere else so I—"

"Decided to take it upon yourself to order something for me that I didn't feel like having," she interrupted.

"You may not want it now. But you can have it later," he said as he looked at his phone once more.

She hated when he got like this. He was consumed with most likely another potential sale. It bothered her that it seemed like more and more Mitchell was seeing people not as human, but as a potential commission for his increasing real estate sales portfolio.

"You know, hon. I think I'm going to go home. I'm tired. I have a lot to do in the next couple of days."

Mitchell suddenly looked up from his phone. "Wait, what?" he said.

Kat began to get up. "I'm going to go home. You're obviously busy. Why don't you go back to the office and finish doing what you're doing and I'll meet you at home?"

"Kat, it wasn't that," he said as he got up

Kat began to walk toward the door. He quickly sprinted behind her. "Wasn't what, Mitch? You asked me to come celebrate, and all night you've been on your phone. It's okay. I get it. You're a popular and great real estate agent. I'll meet you at home," she said as she began to put her coat on.

"Kat, it's not like that," he told her.

"It's okay, babe," she replied as she walked out the door and began to walk down the rainy street. He ran after her.

"Kat, I love you! Marry me," he yelled.

Kat realized that she had forgotten her umbrella at the restaurant. She was soaked from head to toe.

She was stunned and confused. The rain felt like cold pins being thrown at her face. She turned around and looked at him. He looked like a drowned rat who was kneeling in front of everyone in the middle of the sidewalk.

"What?" she said.

"Marry me, Katherine. I'm sorry. Everything that I was planning for the night went wrong. The musicians, the weather." He took out a Cartier box. He opened it up and there was a six-carat pink diamond ring surrounded by diamonds. "I adore you. Everything about you. These last three years have been the best three years of my life. You've taught me so much about people and life. You are one of the most talented and strongest women I know. I am sorry. But I will make it up to you forever and always."

"Mitch, I—"

"Kat, please," Mitchell said walking up to her. He held her hand. "Will you marry me?"

Kat nodded her head. She felt like an idiot. "Yes, I'll marry you," she said.

The crowd that had gathered around the sidewalk clapped as Mitchell placed the ring on Kat's finger and kissed her.

Kat's phone rang through her coat. Mitchell felt the vibrating phone. "Are you going to get that?" He smiled.

She picked it up and noticed that there were a ton of missed calls from her mother. "It's Mom. It's probably about my dad and this interview. Let me answer it," she said as Mitchell held her hand.

"Hello, Mom?" Kat said, answering the phone.

"Kat, where have you been? I've been calling you for hours," her mother responded.

"I've been busy with work. What's going on? We're still surprising Dad, right?" she asked.

"Honey, you need to come home. Your dad has had a heart attack and is in the ICU," her mother cried.

Kat was stunned.

"I'm coming right now," she said.

Chapter 4

As soon as she heard about her father, Kat was on the next flight to Sweetbriar, Georgia. It had been years since she had been home. Maybe six or seven years, at least. As the plane flew her home, her mind flooded with memories about her small town and its townspeople. From fishing in the bay with her friends and family to running to get donuts from McQuayde's Bakery.

Those strawberry jelly donuts, she thought. *Need to grab one the minute I get into town.*

Memories also came back of Jayson McQuayde. Again. He was her childhood sweetheart. They grew up together. In school, they were THE couple. There wasn't anything he wouldn't do for her, or her for him. That is until he slept with this girl, Nicole, who was insanely jealous of her. She could see them both now. Nicole with mousy brown hair that looked like a rat's nest. She and her friends had been nice to Nicole. She had a crap life before she came to Sweetbriar with her mother. Her mom was abused by her father and got into drugs. Nicole was pretty much left on her own to raise not only herself but her siblings. After all Kat did for her, she never thought that Nicole would do that to her. She thought even less of Jayson. They were supposed to go to college together and get married. They had it all planned out. Leaving at the time was the best thing she could have ever done.

The plane touched down on the tarmac. She took out her phone and texted her friend, Thea.

Me: Hey, I'm here.

Thea: Perfect! I'm literally rolling up at the gate.

Me: I can't wait to see you!

Thea: Me too, love!

A few minutes later, after getting her bags, a petite woman with long brown hair stood in front of a blue BMW as Kat made her way to the door.

"Took you long enough," the young woman said to her.

"Thanks for the help, bestie." Kat smirked as she walked over to the woman and hugged her. They hugged each other tight. It had been years. Way too many years. They pulled away from each other and both had tears in their eyes.

"Thea Morales as I live and breathe," Kat said. "You looked fantastic."

Thea wore a pair of designer jeans and a black tee. She could have been a model if she wanted to. But instead, chose to be a fashion designer.

Thea smiled warmly. Her brown eyes twinkled with delight. "So do you. Sorry, that the circumstances aren't the best, babe," Thea told her as she grabbed one of the bags.

"Any word on Daddy? I had my phone turned off."

The two ladies walked over to the back of the car. Thea popped open the trunk and they began to place Kat's bags in the back of her car.

"No change. My mom is with your mom and sisters."

"Aww, that's so sweet."

"They're besties like us." Thea reminded her. "I'm not surprised. My mom, your mom, and Melissa McQuayde."

Kat snickered. "Truth. Speaking of McQuayde? How is—"Kat continued.

"Jacob and I are fine," Thea said. "As for the other? I heard he's out on the injured list."

"Aww, poor little rich boy. I feel so bad for him. Maybe one of the weekly starlets our entertainment reporters talk to can console him in his time of need."

Thea's eyes widened. "Ouch. See there is still no love loss there."

"Never. So how is everyone else?"

"The same. You know Sweetbriar. Nothing changes. Oh, except for Nicole Mattox. Mr. Shooter left her Shooter's bar.

Kat put the last bag in the car and Thea put down the trunk. Her eyes widened with amazement.

"Nicole Mattox? That Nicole?"

Thea nodded. "Yes. Old Man Shooter passed away about a year ago and she's been working there for years as a bartender."

"Oh, wow. He was so nice. Sorry to hear that."

"Remember, that time at school when we both wore some trendy dress and Trina Paige and another girl picked on us and we got into a huge fight?" Thea reminisced.

"Those brand-new dresses were toast. We were so upset that our parents were going to go off. We went into the bar to console our feelings—"

Kat began to laugh and interrupted, "We asked Mr. Shooter for a double and he gave us a shot glass with a part of a chocolate peanut butter milkshake."

Thea laughed. "Remember what he called it?"

Kat laughed. "Milk crack!" they said out together. They continued to laugh.

"We must have been seven or eight," Thea said.

"God, I remember we told him everything that had happened that day. I thought we were in so much trouble. And the next day—"

Kat interrupted, "We both had brand-new dresses. I can't believe he did that. I guess he thought of us as his kids. My mom told me as I got older. We thought everything bad back then was the worst thing that could have happened to us," Kat said.

"Those were some fun times. It's sad when you have to grow up. Sometimes things aren't always what they seem," Thea said.

"Facts," Kat agreed. "I know that all too well."

"Let's get you to the hospital, Kit Kat. Your mom and sisters need you. Your father needs you. We all missed you. Literally, everyone in town can't wait to see you."

Kat nodded. "Definitely home. No one in New York calls me Kit Kat."

"Kit Kat you shall always remain," Thea quipped.

The two got into the car and drove directly to the hospital.

Chapter 5

As Thea got closer to town, the thought of coming home after being gone for so long began to gnaw at her stomach. She was a ball of nerves. Not at seeing her parents or siblings, but everyone else.

She should have never been gone for so long. She looked out the window of the passenger seat and saw Sweetbriar Bay in the distance. It was a beautiful day today. During this time of year, everything should be in full bloom. The peonies, the roses, the lilacs.

The town square must smell heavenly.

"Nearly there," Thea told her.

Kat looked over at her friend. "You're fine. It's not like he's going anywhere. I texted Mom a little while ago. He's stable," Kat said.

"That's good."

"Mom said your mom and Melissa are still there. In fact, Melissa is driving her crazy."

Thea laughed. "Well, that must be genetic. Jake drives me to drink constantly."

"So glad you two are still seeing each other. That's awesome. How long has it been?"

"It's been like fifteen years. Since high school. I adore him though. Even if he's grouchy, a pain in the butt, and a tad neurotic. He's my pain in the butt."

"You got the good twin. I had the evil one."

Thea laughed. "We were the Four Musketeers, back in the day. "

"We sure were. Literally, the squad. I felt like we were unstoppable in high school,"

Kat remembered.

"Those were the days. Fun times at that bay you keep looking at," Thea said.

"That's for sure," Kat agreed as she looked back out the window.

"It's still so beautiful. There used to be this white gorgeous farmhouse that sat right in front of it."

"Oh, the Mulderry Farmhouse!" said Thea

"That's it. Mrs. Mulderry was so nice. We all used to pick strawberries and blueberries at her house. She had the most beautiful gardens. I always wanted that house."

"It's still beautiful. She passed away a couple of years ago. The house apparently is just sitting there," Thea told her.

Kat was in shock. "You're kidding me. What about her kids? No one wanted it? How awful."

Thea shrugged as she continued to drive. "Talk to your mom. I heard there's a For Sale sign up front," Thea informed her as she pulled up to the hospital doors and stopped the car.

"Here we are," said Thea

"You coming in with me?" Kat asked her as she got out of the car.

"I'll be there in a few. Going to find a place to park"

"Okay." Kat nodded and went in.

Thea didn't park the car. She drove up the street to the diner owned by Jacob and his fraternal twin, Jayson McQuayde, called "The Hat Trick."

She needed to give Jacob and Jayson a heads-up that Kat was home. Especially, Jayson. Despite, Kat's hatred of her ex, Thea adored him. He was like a brother to her. There wasn't anything the three of them wouldn't do for each other. Jayson needed to prepare for Kat's wrath. It was coming.

The young fashion designer walked into the diner and up to the front counter. The place was wall-to-wall people since it was lunchtime.

The place was literally a hockey player's dream. It was full of NHL memorabilia. Since Jayson and Jacob both were in the NHL, along with their father. There were tons of photos and celebrity memorabilia all over the place, and Jayson's team colors of red and white. The floor was a replica of a hockey rink. Blue line and all.

"Hey, is Jacob or Jayson here?" Thea asked the young man at the front counter.

"Jake is. I'll go grab him," he told her.

"Thanks."

A few seconds later. A tall man with brown hair and hazel eyes came out of the back. He had an athletic build and wore a dark blue shirt and jeans. His lips pursed into a smile when he saw his longtime love. He leaned over the counter and kissed her.

"Hey you. This is a surprise," Jacob said with a sexy Southern drawl. "You hungry?"

"I am. But it'll have to wait for a bit. I wanted to let you and Jay know that Kat is home. You know her dad had a heart attack. So, I just picked her up and dropped her off at the hospital really quick."

"Oh wow!" Jake said. "I knew her dad was in the hospital from Mom but—"

"She hasn't been home in years."

Jacob nodded. "Literally years. I think like seven or eight, Thea. It was a good day too," he quipped.

Thea lightly hit him on the arm and snickered. "Stop. You know you love her."

"I guess. I'm pissed that she's been gone so long. Geeze. Is being a famous lifestyle guru, or whatever, she is now so important that she can't come home and see everyone?"

Thea shrugged. "I agree. She had tried a few times to come back but something always happened."

"Let's see. Oh, like her interview with the Duchess of Suffolk or going to stay at Martha Stewart's home for a weekend? Why come home to marshland central?" he joked.

"Where's Jayson?" Thea asked.

"He's home. His knee is bothering him today so I told him to stay off of it for a bit. "

"You may want to tell him she's here. He'll eventually run into her and he should be prepared for all hell breaking loose. She already called him the evil one," Thea said.

Jake shook his head. "I wish the hell he would just tell her the damn truth. The shit was years ago. I can't believe it's gone on this long."

"I know. He needs to come clean and end it." Thea sighed as she looked at her watch. "Oh, let me get back to the hospital. I'm supposed to be looking for a parking spot. I'm coming back here for lunch and I'll bring her," she told him as she gave him a kiss.

"Okay, I'll call him now," Jacob replied to her.

"I love you," Thea told him walking out the door.

"Love you too," Jacob said.

Chapter 6

When Kat got to the cardiac ward. The first person she saw was her mother, Claire McKinnon. Her mom was beautiful. Her long hair pulled into a bun. Her brown eyes, despite looking tired, had a twinkle of optimism in them. Her mom was the town's attorney. Not fighting for the people she cared about was not an option. Her husband, who was the family's rock, was no exception. Claire was simply dressed in a pair of blue jeans and a black T-shirt. Kat's eyes filled with tears as she saw her mother, sisters, and grandmother sitting in the lobby.

"Mom!" Kat called as she ran toward her mother.

"Kit Kat!" Claire said, her long arms outstretched.

The two women hugged each other tightly for several seconds. Kat hugged each one of her sisters and grandmother. She hugged her mother's best friends, Melissa McQuayde and Nellie Morales.

"How's Daddy?" Kat asked as she looked around at everyone.

"He's resting. His heart attack was massive. He's in the ICU. We'll know more later. He's a lot better than when he was admitted last night, which is a good sign," Claire told her. "If anyone can pull through this, it's your father."

Kat nodded. "I got on the first plane. God, it's been forever since I've been home."

"Too long," Kat's grandmother, Mae, told her.

"I agree, Grandma. I thought I'd have forever."

Mae McKinnon was the matriarch of the family. Her family meant everything to her. She was born and raised in Sweetbriar. She knew everyone in town. She was respected and beloved. Her short silver hair and sharp wit showed that she could more than hold her own at seventy-nine years old. Like her son and granddaughter, she had the gift of words. She had founded the town's newspaper, *The Sweetbriar Post*, after seeing illiterate family members and friends not knowing what was happening in town. She had always hoped that Kat would want to take over the newspaper one day. She was saddened after she had graduated college in New York, that she never came home. Until today.

Mae walked over to her granddaughter and held her hand.

"*The Sweetbriar Post* is going to need some help, Kit Kat."

"Help? Isn't the paper doing well, Grandma?" Kat asked her grandmother.

Mae let out a huge sigh as she looked over at her daughter-in-law.

"Kat, there's some cash flow issues with *The Post*. Subscriptions are down, advertising isn't the way it used to be," Claire explained.

"I told your father that we could sell the paper. There have been several offers over the years," Mae said.

"When the worst of this is over, your father is going to need to rest. Before this heart attack, he was at *The Post* twelve to fourteen hours a day, six days a week," Claire said.

Kat was in shock. That paper was her father's entire life. He would never sell it. It meant too much to him.

"Daddy will never allow *The Post* to be sold, Grandma. Mom, we can't do that to him. That will kill him."

They all looked sadly at Kat. Thea came running into the lobby.

"Sorry, parking was crazy," she told all of them as she walked over and gave her mother a kiss on the cheek as well as Claire, Mae, and Melissa.

"Any word?" she asked.

"He's resting. He had some tests earlier. We're just waiting to hear the results," Claire said.

"Praying for good news," Thea replied.

As she said that, the doctor walked into the lobby and walked toward Claire.

"Mrs. McKinnon, got the results back. His condition has improved over the last twenty-four hours. He will make a full recovery but he's in for a long road. Lots of rest, lots of physical therapy. A change in lifestyle."

"Got it," Claire said.

"No more Hat Trick double bacon cheeseburgers at midnight," the doctor warned her.

"Oh, Dad!" Kat said.

"Or eating chocolate and banana cream cheese puffs I make at the bakery," said Melissa.

"Good Lord," Mae said.

"Or those triple cheese quesadillas we have at the restaurant," Nellie added.

"Wow," Thea said. "He eats all of that stuff?"

"All of those guys do," Claire said.

"Every single day. Weekends are worse. When my husband and your fathers get together. It's like a damn fraternity," Melissa said

"It's a wonder we've never had to bail them out of jail," Claire stated.

"Well," Mae said. "There was this one time—"

Claire interrupted, "I don't want to know, Mae."

Kat shook her head. "Some things never change," she observed.

"Well, it's going to have to now," Claire said.

"He can't work at the paper for a while. We all love *The Post* here in town but is there anyone who can help out for a bit?" the doctor said.

"I can for a few days," Kat volunteered.

"I can see if Ian will help out Kat," Melissa said.

"Oh, the other prodigal son is home?" Kat asked

"Yeah, he's been back for about a year. Leaving a trail of crazy along the way," Melissa informed.

"But he's a great reporter. I'll see if I can find him from under his rock later," Kat said.

"Good luck on that. He's thirty-five and he stresses me the hell out," Melissa explained. "He's not like the twins or Kelly."

"The twins are worse, dear," Claire teased.

"You're probably right. It's a wonder my husband and I aren't in rehab from these kids. They're adults and they are worse now than they were as kids. How is that possible?"

"We wouldn't love them if we didn't worry a little, Melissa. Doesn't matter how old they are. They are always our babies," Mae said. "Look at mine in the ICU."

"We'll be moving him into a private room later. When we do that, we'll start to let all of you in there to see him. He's going to be okay," the doctor reassured.

"Thank you, Doc," Mae said.

"Of course, Mae," he replied as he walked away.

"Thank God, he's going to be okay," Kat said.

Her mother sat down and put her head in her hands. "Thank God. Thank you for letting him live. Now, we all need to come together to help him get some rest. I don't want him stressing about that newspaper anymore."

"Don't worry, Mom. I can stay for a few days and help out with the paper," Kat said.

"What about your interview with Jacques Primeau?" her mother asked

"I can do that from here. It's no big deal. That interview will be an amazing surprise for Daddy when he gets home."

Claire looked up and smiled at her daughter.

"He'd like that, sweetheart," Claire told her.

"Since none of us can see him until he moves into his new room, I'll go home, get something to eat, and change," Kat said.

"I'll take you to get something to eat and home," Thea volunteered.

Chapter 7

Thea and Kat decided to get something to eat. Kat hadn't eaten anything since before her flight. She was hungry and tired. It'd be awhile before they moved her father from the ICU so why not grab some food, take a shower, and get some rest.

Thea pulled into the local diner called, The Hat Trick.

"Hey, is this place new?" Kat asked.

"Yes, it is. Jacob and Jayson took it over about six months ago. Mel retired."

"Good for him!" Kat said. "Did you say Jayson owns the diner?"

Thea turned toward her friend in the passenger seat. "Yes. He's not here though. He's an investor. In fact, Ian partially owns it too. It's like some McQuayde brotherly pact. They each own a third. Is this an issue for you because there's a McDonald's up the street," Thea said, pursing her lips.

"No, it's fine. I haven't seen Jake in a while. Jayson is probably in the city."

Thea's lips curved into a smile.

"That's my girl. Let's go and have some food. Jake makes the BEST veggie burgers in the state."

"Yum! Let's go," Kat said as she got out of the car.

She liked what they did to the old diner. It went from being a run-down, gray greasy spoon to a thriving, upscale, red-and-white diner with a hockey stick in front of the neon sign.

She was impressed with the full parking lot.

"Damn, packed house," she told Thea.

"It always is," Thea explained. "The guys did a complete overhaul of the old diner and upgraded everything. Wait until you see the inside."

The two of them went in. Kat looked around at all the hockey memorabilia, including a Stanley Cup replica at the far end of the diner.

The McQuayde's had a long-standing history in the NHL. So, it was no secret or surprise that they would want to do something hockey related in the town they were raised in. Jacob and Jayson followed their father, Dennis, into playing hockey. Dennis was an NHL legend, who parlayed his talents from the rink to a lucrative endorsement contract and an NHL news analyst on TV. Jacob suffered a career-ending injury early in his career. Instead of following in his father's footsteps, he hated the spotlight, he decided to enjoy a low-key life here in town with his longtime girlfriend, Thea. Jacob's fraternal twin brother, Jayson, was another story. He lived and breathed hockey all day long. It was no surprise that he would be good enough to play in the NHL or even become one of the league's biggest stars. He was talented, handsome, and charming. His charm won Kat over. They were high school sweethearts for years. They were inseparable until he found out that he was an early draft pick to the New York All Stars.

He became cocky, rude, and flirted with everything that walked.

As Kat looked at the early photos of Jayson, she remembered how happy he was when she got the news that she got into Syracuse University on a full scholarship. He was, at one time, her biggest supporter. He would sit there and listen to her go on about the world and how she wanted to tell people's stories with her writing, like her father and grandmother did.

He told her that she should. She couldn't leave him or Thea or her life here. Jayson was going to college here at the time. She nearly decided to turn down the scholarship until she found him in bed with Nicole that night.

She left for Syracuse the next day.

Seeing him on the wall and how much he had accomplished brought back everything. She was hurt, angry, and missed him. He had done well for himself. Too bad he had to change to do it.

"Looking at memories?" Thea said, coming up behind her.

Kat nodded as she looked at Jayson's photos. "He's a talented man. I'll give him that. He would get up every day and go to the indoor rink before anyone was up and practice. Every, single day. Hockey is like taking a damn vitamin for him."

"He's out with a knee injury right now. Did you hear that?" Thea said.

Kat turned to her friend. Her eyes filled with sadness. "He is, really?"

Thea nodded. "Yeah."

Kat's brief sadness turned back into slight anger. "Too bad. Karma is a bitch."

Thea rolled her eyes. "Come on Kat, really?"

"Sorry, Thea. Maybe he should have something to fall back on."

"Um, he invested into this diner so I think he does?" Thea answered back.

"True. He can be soothed by one of those actress girlfriends he has on his arm. I swear it's a different chick every week," Kat snapped.

"He can do what he wants, Kat."

"I'm aware, Thea."

"It's been years. Every time there is a mention of him or a photo, this shit happens. It's exhausting," Thea snapped back.

Kat took a deep breath. Her friend was right. Why should they get snippy with each other because of one person?

"You're right. Let's get some food. It's probably why I'm so grumpy," Kat said.

Thea wrapped her arms around her friend. "Yes!" Thea said.

They found a booth and opened up a menu. A few seconds later, Jacob came over with two glasses and some water.

"What can I get you, ladies?" he asked.

Thea smiled warmly at her boyfriend.

"You know what I want," she quipped. Jacob gave her a kiss. "If we weren't in a public place. I would, but... I'll grab you a veggie burger and sweet potato fries," he whispered.

"Deal," she said.

"Kat!" Jacob said, running over to her side of the table to give her a hug.

"Hello!" Kat said.

"Welcome home, sweetheart. How's your dad?"

"He's doing better. They're moving him from the ICU right now. So, we figured we'd grab some food and I'd go home for a bit and change. Nice place!"

"Thank you! It was a lot of work, but we love how it turned out."

Jacob looked around at the busy diner. "What can I get you?" he asked her.

"I'll have what Thea's having. That veggie burger looks amazing."

"It's fantastic! You'll love it!" Thea told her.

"Two veggie burgers and sweet potato fries coming up. How long are you in town for?" Jacob asked

"A few days until Dad gets on his feet. By the way, is your older brother, Ian, around?" Kat asked.

"He should be at *The Post*. He came in for breakfast this morning."

"Oh cool. I'll go later."

"Be right back with your orders," Jacob said as he walked away.

Kat smiled. "Aww, it's good to see him!"

"He adores you." Thea said.

"I adore him. It's good to be home," Kat admitted. Kat looked down at her purse and around the diner.

"Hey, I need to go to the ladies' room," she said as she got up.

"Oh, okay. It's still in the same spot," Thea instructed.

"Okay," Kat said as she quickly turned around. She continued to look at her phone when she went barreling into someone.

Plates and glasses went flying. The food went all over her T-shirt and white jeans.

"What the?" she said. She looked up and then she saw him.

She was incensed.

Chapter 8

Kat was livid. Her white designer jeans and shirt were covered in gravy, soda, ketchup, and mustard.

He stood across from her. He hadn't changed it a bit. He was tall with hazel eyes and short brown hair. Jayson seemed bemused at what he saw.

"Well, look who I literally ran into," he quipped.

She screamed, "You asshole!"

Jayson laughed. "Good to see you too, Kit Kat. How ya doing?"

"I hate you! What the hell are you doing here?" she said, as someone came over and gave her a couple of towels to wipe herself off.

Jayson had food all over him as well. He gave one of the staff a couple of the dishes and took one of the towels and began to wipe himself off. To him, she hadn't changed at all. She was still this petite, little powerhouse. Angry, but a force.

"In case you didn't know. I co-own this place," he told her. "I should ask you the same question?"

She wiped some food off of her chest.

"Dad had a heart attack. So, I came home to see how he is. Your mom was at the hospital with my mother."

Jayson's mischievous grin turned to sadness. "I'm sorry. I didn't—"

Kat interrupted, "I don't feel like doing this right now, Jayson. I just wanted to get something to eat and change." She gave him the towel and turned to Thea, who was stunned.

"I think I want to go home, Thea."

Thea nodded as she got up. "I'll get our food to go."

Kat walked out the door.

Thea walked over to Jayson with surprise.

35

"What are you doing here? Didn't Jake call you?"

Jayson looked confused. "Call me about what?"

"That she was home! He told me that you weren't going to be in today," Thea said.

"Well, my knee was feeling better thanks to physical therapy today. I can't believe she's still pissed."

"You need to fess up, Jay. This is ridiculous. Especially now, due to her dad."

"Thea, that was so long ago. It was the right thing to do at the time. She wouldn't have left otherwise."

"You need to tell her the truth. You know people in this town talk. She's going to find out from someone sooner or later," Thea said.

"What do I even say? Did you see that? She barely could look at me."

"Tell her the truth, Jayson. Tell her that you didn't sleep with Nicole. Tell her that you did it so she could go to Syracuse and not go here to State," Thea pointed out.

Jayson took a deep breath. He continued to wipe himself off with the towel as his fraternal twin brother Jacob brought out the bags and observed the mess as it was being cleaned up.

"I see Hurricane Kat was here," Jacob quipped.

"She always has to make a damn entrance," Jayson complained.

Jacob laughed. "I bet you loved every minute of it. "

"Well, she did look cute, even with all that food spilled on her," Jayson said.

Thea punched Jayson in his arm. He was like a brother to her, despite of how her best friend felt about him. "You're ridiculous," she said, grabbing the two bags and walking out the door.

Jacob looked at his brother and shook his head.

"What?" Jayson shrugged.

"I warned you that she was home. What are you doing here?"

"Well, someone had to do payroll. And PT went great so I came in to look after our diner."

"I could have done payroll, you know. I do it most of the time. Since you play nine months out of the year," Jacob reminded him.

Jayson looked out the door at Kat. She was talking to Thea. She looked distraught, tired, and angry.

"I had to see her, Jake. Even if she was pissed at me. I had to see her."

"Listen, I don't know how long she's home for, but Thea is right. You need to end this shit and now. It's stupid that it's even gone on this long. Saying this to you as your twin and best friend. End it. However it ends. Even if she hates your ass, which she may even more than she does now. End it," Jacob told Jason.

Outside Kat was a ball of nerves. She didn't know how to think or feel. The last forty-eight hours had been a crazy mix of emotions and she was done. She got the interview of a lifetime, she was engaged to a great guy, her father had a massive heart attack, and now she saw an ex-flame that she thought she would marry one day. Every time she saw him, she got angry.

"You okay?" Thea asked.

Kat nodded. "Yes, I'm fine. Just a lot. I was not ready for that."

Thea sighed. "I tried to warn him that you were home."

Kat rolled her eyes. "You warned him? What, about me? What's he doing home, Thea? Hockey season is still in full swing."

"You had a lot on your mind due to your dad, remember I said he injured his knee? I was actually going to tell you later that he was home."

"I forgot. He should have injured his ass," Kat said.

"Come on, Kat. How long are you going to punish him? You haven't been home in years."

"As long as I want to. He devastated me when he slept with that whore," Kat said.

"And look at you now. You're a successful writer and reporter. You have a rich, new guy." Thea looked at Kat's hand. "And what is that on your finger?"

Kat showed her the ring on her left hand. "Mitchell proposed to me last night."

Thea's eyes widened with surprise, "Oh, my God! That's fantastic!" Thea hugged her friend. "Does anyone else know?"

Kat shook her head. "Nope. You're the first."

"I won't say anything. You have enough going on right now."

"You're right. I have a great life. All of that was so long ago. But when I see him and since I've been home, I remember how all of us were back then. You, me, Jake, Jayson. We were going to take over the world. Jay and I were going to get married and he was going to play for the Rangers. I would be a mom and write books."

Thea smiled. "You have more to offer the world than that," she told her.

"But it was what I wanted at the time. And things happened. It was probably for the best. I found my voice with my stories and I have a good life in the city."

"Sounds like it."

"Mitchell is great. He's this superstar real estate agent. You didn't meet him when you were in town. It's too bad, you would like him."

"I'm sure I'll meet him," Thea said.

Kat nodded with tears in her eyes. "Yeah. Let's go."

The two of them got into the car and went to Kat's childhood home.

Chapter 9

After a shower, some food, and a nap, Kat felt more like herself again. It was a nice feeling being in her old bedroom. It was safe, comfy, and all Kat. It was still in the same colors of light purple and white. But her mom took down the old posters of Leonardo DiCaprio and high school banners. They did keep up all her family photographs with her and her sisters, Thea, Jacob, and Jayson.

I'll never be able to get away from you. Will I? she thought as she looked at the photos of the two of them together. They were both fresh-faced, without an ounce of worry for what life had ahead. Those times were innocent, fun, and carefree.

She changed into a pair of black jeans and a light purple sleeveless sweater with matching flats. She combed her long, wavy hair and placed it into a ponytail.

Thea had left her a few hours ago. It was now two o'clock. She figured that Ian should be at *The Post* by now since lunch hour usually ended at one and he should be back working on his stories.

She walked through the beautifully decorated home and saw a note from her grandmother Mae on the counter.

"Kat, if you are home, you'll need these. Love, Grandma."

She left a pair of car keys.

Kat smiled. She couldn't believe it. She walked toward the garage and opened the garage door. Her old white, VW bug convertible sitting there looking amazing.

She got in and began to laugh. Her high school tassels were still on the rearview mirror along with a JM + KM 4 ever sticker they made in art class. She was in shock that they kept her car. Since she lived in the city, she really didn't need it. She used the public transit. She placed

39

the keys into the ignition, and it started immediately. She squealed. She slowly let down the convertible top and drove off toward *The Post*.

As she drove through the town, she realized that despite seeing a Starbucks, the other main stores throughout the town had stayed the same. Sweetbriar was a picturesque town. There were trees that lined the clean streets. Everyone's lawns were manicured and perfectly landscaped. On this early spring day, tulips bordered the grounds and the lilacs were in full, fragrant bloom. As she pulled up to *The Sweetbriar Post*, she smiled. It was literally her second home. As she got out, people walked by her, welcoming her home. "Welcome home, Kat."

"Thank you, Mr. Greenfield," she said.

"Kat, welcome home!" another person said walking by *The Post*.

Kat smiled. "Thank you so much," she said. She walked through the main doors and ran into Lois at reception. Lois was a lovely relic from years past. Her father and family adored her. She ran the desk and knew everyone who came and went into the building. She ordered the supplies and also helped management with the books. She was a short woman with spiky white hair and blue eyes. She always wore the brightest of colors. Today she had on a lime green dress. Lois was one of her grandmother's closest friends.

"Lois!" Kat said, running over to her grandmother's dear friend.

Lois got up and went over to her. "Well, I'll be! Kat McKinnon as I live and breathe," Lois said.

The two ladies embraced. "When did you get in?" Lois asked.

"Early this morning. How are you?" Kat asked.

"Pretty good, all things considered. We are all so concerned about your dad."

"Oh, I know. Did Mom or Grandma keep y'all posted?"

"Yes. I heard they're moving him?" Lois said.

"Yes, they are. They're moving him to another room. If they haven't done it already. I figured while they were doing that, I would check on things here for her and Grandma."

Lois grabbed her hand. "This paper is bleeding money, sweetie. Your father owes people all kinds of money."

"What?" Kat said.

"Come. I'll have you talk with accounts receivable and the comptroller's office." Lois said.

They walked to accounts receivable. Kat asked to see the books.

After looking through them for a couple of hours and a talk with the comptroller, she couldn't believe the amount of businesses in town that owed her father money and vice versa.

"Your dad is in debt for over 250,000," the comptroller said. "Now, he did get loans and is current. But with him out right now, and not getting enough advertisers, I told your grandmother that maybe looking at a new owner is an option. That way, your family wouldn't be losing any more money and *The Post* would be in a strategic position to be one of the best papers in Georgia."

"This paper is my family's legacy and my father's life. This paper isn't for sale nor will it be sold," Kat said. "You mentioned advertisers? Is there a reason why these people aren't paying my dad?"

The comptroller, who was this middle-aged man with glasses and gray hair, shrugged. "Excuses. Honestly, he's too nice," Lois agreed.

"He'll let some people get ads in exchange for a meal or a free car wash."

Kat's eyes raised. "What! Is he insane? Grandma never did that. What is he thinking?"

"He's not," Lois said. "He's too nice. Your grandmother has told him. I have, the comptroller..."

"So stubborn," the comptroller said. "If we can get advertisers for the Harvest Festival and make some other changes. This can be solved. The good news is that *The Post* has a lot of assets. The building is paid for, as is all the equipment. All the equipment is also up-to-date as well.

"Is *The Post* in mobile form yet? We can probably get more digital advertisers that way."

"It isn't. *The Post* doesn't even have a Friendsbook page," Lois said.

"Well, let's get started," Kat responded. "How long will it take to fix everything?" she asked the comptroller.

"About six months if we get a plan together," he told her.

"Then we got work to do. I'll see if I can get some advertisers and some help."

"We also lost one of our sports reporters recently. Left for a higher paying market," Lois said.

"Then we hire another person," Kat replied. "Anything else?"

"Ian is out today working on a series for Founders' Day," Lois informed her.

"Founders' Day is typically an advertisers' dream around here. Who do we have so far?"

"McQuayde's Bakery and your mother's law office," Lois confirmed.

"Seriously? Where is everyone else? The Hat Trick? Shooter's? The Sweetbriar Inn, the Starbucks? "

"I know," Lois said.

"We got work to do," Kat said. "Guess I'm staying more than a few days."

Chapter 10

After her meeting with *The Post's* comptroller, the accounts receivable department, and her grandmother's former assistant/receptionist, Lois, Kat realized that she was going to need to get a strategy together.

She sat in her father's office that was in the corner of the newsroom. It was a nice office with a window that overlooked the town square. There were photos of their family sprinkled throughout the office, along with achievement awards. Her father, prior to when he took over *The Post*, had a storied journalism career himself. He wrote for such publications as *Time* and *Life*. In fact, he met Kat's mother while doing a story on a civil rights case in Atlanta.

It was odd to be sitting at the desk. Her grandmother sat there before her father and now she sat here.

It wouldn't be long, but she felt she had to keep *The Post* going. Her grandmother didn't sacrifice everything in order for her family to lose this. It was their legacy.

Who did she know that could help her? She could set up a meeting with the advertising department and see if they could come up with some promotional campaigns. The circulation department could help her with why subscribers were dropping. And then there was the news department.

As she looked around, there was no hustle and bustle like she remembered in years past. Most of the reporters she knew were long gone. Her grandmother mentioned that Ian McQuayde, Jayson and Jacob's older brother, was their star reporter. The last time Kat was home seven years ago, there were several.

Where should she start? She looked out the door of the newsroom and watched as people walked around and talked on their cell phones, while occasionally typing on their computers.

She picked up the phone and called her boss, Ross, at the *Empire Post.*

"Hello?" the deep, rich English tone asked.

"Hey, Ross, it's me Kat."

"Ah, Katherine. How is your father?" he asked.

"He's doing better. They are moving him from the ICU to his own room. I'm waiting until he's all settled before I go back to the hospital."

"When is your interview with Jacques?" Ross asked.

"It's tomorrow morning. Going to do it here and transmit it to you when I'm done."

"Sounds like a plan," Ross said.

"Ross, I need some advice. *The Post* here is struggling. Advertisers have been literally bartering services from Dad while the paper is hemorrhaging money as a result."

"How bad?"

"At least a quarter of a million dollars."

Ross let out a huge groan on the phone. "That's not good."

"Well, one good thing is that we have a lot of assets. We own everything. The building, the printing presses, the computers, all of that. It's getting people to subscribe and retain the readers we have, that's another one of the issues."

"Why did your father do that? Your grandmother is an icon. She must be livid," Ross told her.

"I wish I knew. It's as if Dad literally gave up doing any kind of business dealings. Grandma has been too focused on my dad's well-being that I don't even think she knows the full scope of what's going on. She did say there were several companies that were willing to buy *The Post.*"

"Of course there are. That paper is one of the best in the South. *The Post* was a beacon during the civil rights era. Your father was a superstar. I would read his stories along with your grandmother's and just be in awe. I would joke to my wife and tell them that I wanted to be like your dad when I grew up."

Kat laughed.

"Aww. He's a great guy. In business, not so much. Anyway, after I write the Jacques Primeau story, I'm going to need to take a few months off to see if I can fix things around here. I won't let my grandmother sell this paper. She'd regret it and that would kill Daddy. And me."

"You know, I do have a bunch of time off to take," Ross said. "Why don't I come down there and help you?"

Kat was in shock. "Oh, Ross, it's okay. You have the *Empire Post* to run."

"The *Empire Post* can literally run itself at this point. I don't mind, Kat. We have a ton of people who are more than capable of running things. I haven't taken a proper sabbatical in years. Give me a couple of days and I'll be there."

"But—" Kat tried to say and Ross interrupted.

"We'll fix this. I'll see you soon," Ross said as he ended the call.

Kat put her head down on the desk. Her mind was spinning from everything.

"Sleeping on the job?" a male voice said to her. She looked up and there was Ian McQuayde standing in front of the desk. Like his younger brothers, he was tall and handsome with shaggy, brown hair. He had an athletic build and had on a pair of jeans and a short-sleeved dress shirt. His eyes were like his father's, a piercing blue. He was a striking man, who literally made every woman in town do a double take.

"Ian McQuayde, I'll be damned," Kat said with a smile.

"How the heck are you?" He walked over to the desk and hugged her.

"I'm good. I'm just looking over Dad's stuff and trying to make sense of it."

Ian shook his head. "Good luck on that. How is the boss man?"

"Doing better," she said.

Ian smiled and sighed. "Thank God. I was the one who called 911."

"Oh, it was you?"

"Yeah, the other day he was so stressed about the budget and staff cuts that he was arguing with everyone."

"He was going to cut staff?"

Ian shrugged and sat down on the front of the desk.

"Sounded like it. Listen, if you need to cut salary, you guys can cut mine. I have enough between me investing in the diner and my savings that I'm okay."

"You're the last person I'd cut. I've been following your stories from the city. Ian, you are a great reporter. My God, that story you did about the homeless woman was amazing. How is she by the way?"

Ian smiled. "She's doing well. Jayson saw the story and not only found the lady's older children. But they all now live in town. She's renting a nice place and the guys hired her as the day manager at the diner."

Kat smiled. "See, these are the stories that *The Post* is known for. That's what *The Post* is about."

"I love it. Always have. This job doesn't even feel like a job," Ian said.

"Got any ideas about how we can drive business?" Kat asked.

"I got a few. Founders' Day is coming up. The Harvest Festival too. The paper could align themselves as a sponsor and run a promotion for subs?"

"Good ones. We need to be online. We are literally the only paper in the South that doesn't have an online presence," she told him.

"Well, I know of someone who can help with that. He owes me a favor."

Kat was relieved. Maybe between her, Ian, and Ross there was a way to fix everything. She hoped.

Chapter 11

Sweetbriar Bay-Summer 2008

Jayson, Kat, Jacob, and Thea were at the bay hanging out. It was summer and it was already eighty-five degrees at 11 a.m. The bay was packed full of teens. It was the day after finals and for the Four Musketeers as they were called, their last final exams ever for Sweetbriar High.

While Thea and Kat laid out in their bikinis with some of the other girls in their class. The boys were wakeboarding.

"Thank God school is over!" Thea said.

"Oh my God, right? I could sleep for a week. My brain is so fried," Kat agreed

"If I never see another algebra equation, it will be too soon," Thea said.

"Amen, girl. All I want to do this summer is have fun!" Kat said as she lay on her back.

"Me too!"

"You know, we need to have a party. One last big blowout with everyone before everyone goes their separate ways," Kat suggested

"Good idea. Where should we have it?" Thea asked.

"We should do it here at the bay. Everyone already hangs out here. We don't have to worry about waiting until parents leave and all that."

Thea nodded. "I dig it."

Kat turned around to her other friends. "How about everyone else?"

Everyone else nodded in agreement.

"Nice. So, a party it is," the girls squealed.

"Hey, y'all cheering for us, babe?" Jayson yelled as he walked up along the shore.

Kat smirked. "Nah, we were planning a party." she informed him.

The two of them forgot that there were others around them. He could gaze into her eyes forever and never get tired of it.

"Nice! Something cool needs to happen around here," Jayson told her.

"That's what I said. We earned it. All the late nights studying, the tutoring, interning at the paper, you working at the bakery, hockey practice."

Jayson rolled his eyes. "If I have to eat another jelly donut, I'm going to go crazy."

Kat laughed. " Aww, I love your mom's jelly donuts," she told him. His fingers weaved into her fingers. He put her hand up to his lips and kissed her hand gently. "Kit Kat, I say this with all the love in my heart for you. But, you're not the one that has to wake up at 3 a.m. to make those damn things every day."

Kat looked at him sadly. "Oh, babe, I'm sorry."

"And people wonder why I fell asleep in algebra?" he told her.

"Well, Miss Reynolds is boring. It doesn't help that she's got that monotone voice either," Thea said.

Kat shrugged. "She's not wrong. That lady can put anyone to sleep. The equation to the problem is..." Kat mocked.

Jayson chuckled. "I guess," he said. "So, did you hear about Syracuse?" he asked Kat.

Kat nodded. "Not yet. I sent in my application late. If I get in, it'll probably be for the winter semester," Kat explained to him. "I figured in the meantime, I could go to Georgia State for the fall and hang out with a certain guy I like."

"Aaah, I see. But I think you are too talented for Georgia State," he told her as he still held her hand.

"I don't know. I just want to be wherever you are. I'd miss you and everyone here too much. We'll see," she responded.

He kissed her on the top of her forehead.

"We'll all be here when you do something that's called a visit. You know, where after you've been gone for a long time, you come home and see your best friends and boyfriend for a certain length of time?" he quipped

"Ha, Ha," she said to him.

"Listen, you and me. This is it. We are it, Kat. Whatever happens and wherever you go, I'll wait. I'm all in," he told her.

"Me too." Kat smiled. He bent over and gave her a kiss.

"Jay! You here?" Ian yelled as he slammed the door behind him.

Jayson immediately woke up. He had fallen fast asleep on the couch with an ice pack on his knee.

While he was home healing from his knee injury, he was staying at his older brother Ian's apartment that was across the street from Shooter's Bar. The sudden door slam not only got him out of his slumber,but reminded him to look for another place to rent with some privacy and soon.

"I'm here," Jayson told Ian. He held his head in his hands. He was trying to get his bearings straight as Ian came through the room and sat down as if there was a hurricane outside.

"Dude, you know Kat's home? I just talked to her. She looks great!" Ian said.

Jayson leaned back on the couch. "Yes, I did. I literally ran into her at the diner."

"How did that go?"

Jayson snickered. "Not well. She and I got food all over each other. She hates me, Ian."

Ian raked his hand through his wavy hair. "Why don't you just come clean and tell her what really happened?"

"What does it matter now? It's been years," Jayson said.

"I take it I wasn't the only one who told you this?" Ian smirked.

"No, you weren't. Listen, she's got a lot on her mind right now. The last thing I want to do is cause her anymore grief."

"But this wouldn't cause grief. She'd probably wind up forgiving you and none of us would have to walk on eggshells to make sure the two of you avoid each other," Ian said.

"She'll be gone in a couple of days anyway, Ian. Let's just let this go. Okay?"

"Um, I think she'll be here more than a couple of days. She's going to help out at *The Post* while her dad recuperates."

Jayson closed his eyes in agony. He couldn't believe what he was hearing.

"How long is that for?"

Ian shrugged. "A few months, at least. She's at the hospital visiting her dad right now."

"Maybe I should go back to New York," Jayson said.

"Running away? God forbid you tell her the truth. This is so stupid. What do you think she'll do to you?"

"It's not that," Jayson denied.

"Then what—" Ian asked.

"I can't see her disappointed in me again. When I saw her for those few minutes today, she was disgusted. She could barely look at me. Before you came in, I was dreaming about how things used to be. I would always tell her that whatever we did, I'd be all in. It was us together, I'd do anything for her. I did what I had to do that day; she wouldn't have left if I hadn't."

"There's always another way, man," Ian said.

Chapter 12

"It is so good to see you, Daddy." Kat said to her father, Michael, in his private hospital room.

Michael's face was tired. He had been through a lot. He had brown eyes and dark brown hair. His stocky build was now covered with blankets and a hospital gown. His eyes were filled with sadness.

"I'm sorry, Kit Kat. I didn't mean to scare anyone."

Kat was sitting next to her father. She held his hand. "Don't do it again. Mom and Grandma are a wreck." she informed him.

"How are your sisters?" he asked.

"They're fine. They are waiting to see you. I'm not going to stay long."

"How long are you in town for?" he asked.

"Until you are back on your feet. Why didn't you tell us about all the issues with *The Post*?"

"It was my fault. I got myself into this mess. I'll get us out," he said. "I don't know what I was thinking. I just figured that people were going to do the right thing."

"Never assume. You taught me that. You were the maverick who didn't take crap. You and Mom always taught us to fight for what we believe in."

Tears filled his eyes. "I got the paper into this. I don't know how to get us out," he admitted.

"I got some ideas. I don't want you to worry about that. There are things we can do. We aren't going to sell the paper. "

"What do you have planned?" Michael asked.

"Well, *The Post* finally goes digital, that's the first thing. Next thing is do some promotional sections for Founders' Day and the Harvest

Festival. Those two in particular should be great for *The Post*. Founders' Day alone should do well. I have some other ideas about online advertising. Since I do influencer ads for my own Instagram account, we could set up a section of our advertising department just for online advertising and marketing."

Michael nodded. "Sounds interesting. Ahead of my time. People around here don't know a lot about the internet or reading a newspaper online, Kat."

"The circulation department's data says differently. I saw the report. We are losing subscriptions because people want a quicker way to read their news sometimes. Ian says he knows someone who can develop an app for phones and other devices, and we can also make sure that *The Post* is on Friendsbook."

MICHAEL LOOKED AT HIS daughter strangely. "What's Friendsbook?" he asked.

"A social media app where friends and family post updates on how they're doing, places they go, etc. Businesses post there as well. *The Post* would do well there. My paper in the city is on there. It's actually how my articles got so popular," she said.

Michael smiled. "So proud of you, Kat. You are doing so well. Every time we see you on TV, we all smile. I can't imagine you would have gotten as far as you have if you stayed here."

"Well, Syracuse was great to me," she told him.

"It was my alma mater too."

"But it's good to be home. I can't believe the last time I was home was seven years ago. It's like the town stayed the same in a way. Sure, some things are different like the new diner and a Starbucks. But everything else? The bay, the magnolia trees, the lilac bushes that are literally in front of your office window..." she said.

"Heavenly scent. Especially, this time of year," he said.

Kat nodded. "Yes. But now, you'll have a bunch of time to rest and start a new lifestyle."

Michael groaned, "Grrr. "

Kat laughed. "No more banana cream puffs, apparently."

"Or double Hat Trick bacon burgers at midnight," her mother Claire said as she walked in.

"I can't believe you did that," Kat said.

"And he would come home and eat a full course meal," Claire pointed out.

"But those burgers are so good," Michael said.

"So are their veggie burgers," Kat pointed out.

Michael shook his head and replied, "Eww."

"They are good. I'm impressed with how well Jacob has done with the diner. Grossman's was falling down," Kat said.

"Jayson, Jacob, and Ian sank a lot of money into that place. They literally gutted it and made it into what it is now," Michael stated.

"All three did a great job," Claire said.

"Well, two probably did the work, while the other collected his millions skating around, dating any and everyone with a pulse."

Claire laughed. "Oh boy. Have you seen him yet?" she asked.

"Yes, and I have the stained jeans and shirt from where he barreled into me as a souvenir of our few minutes together."

Michael laughed. "I needed to see that."

"He's still one of the cockiest human beings that I have ever met," Kat grumbled. "He didn't even say sorry or ask if I was okay."

"You probably didn't give him a chance to say anything," Claire said.

"Don't stick up for him, Mom."

"His mother is my best friend. His father is your father's best friend. Just because you have issues with him doesn't mean the rest of us do.

Jayson's a great guy. It's time for you to stop this nonsense and talk to him," Claire declared.

"If you are really going to be here for a while; you're going to see him eventually. Talk it out, Kat. You have a boyfriend and a great life in New York. Why are you so hung up on him?" her father asked

"We didn't have closure," she told her parents.

"Then have it now. Before you won't be able to," Michael said.

Kat looked over at her mother.

"He's right. Talk to him."

Kat nodded her head in agreement. "You're right. It's time to deal with this," she said.

Chapter 13

A few days later, Kat rolled up to the old home she loved as a child on Mulderry Street.

It was a beautiful white farmhouse that sat several feet from the bay. The home, while still beautiful, had lost some of its grandeur.

The white picket fence that surrounded the property was now battered with some of the posts broken. The covered porch needed to be cleaned up, the grass was overgrown.

But it was still beautiful.

She'd need a place to stay while she helped out at *The Post* and staying with her parents while her father recuperated was not an option.

A few minutes later, another car pulled up next to her. It was her friend, Candace, who was now a real estate agent in town.

Candace was a gorgeous tall woman, with long black hair and green eyes. She wore a black halter dress with black sandals.

Candace was always a good friend to Kat and Thea growing up. They shared the same tastes and had a great time. She was kind and generous. Kat wasn't surprised when she found out that Candace turned out to be a real estate agent. Her personality fit the profession to a T.

Kat grinned when she saw her friend get out of her Mercedes convertible.

"Candace Brighton!" Kat squealed.

Candace smiled widely. She ran over to her friend and gave her a massive hug.

"You mean Candace Brighton-Stafford," Candace corrected.

Kat chuckled. "So, you're married! When did this happen?"

"Two years ago tomorrow," Candace said as she flashed her large five-carat diamond engagement ring and matching wedding band.

"Well, congrats and Happy Anniversary. I got one of those beauties myself," Kat told her, flashing the engagement ring Mitchell gave her.

"Oh, Kat! That's fantastic. Who's the lucky guy?"

"Well, he's like you. He's in real estate. His name is Mitchell Simmons."

"Wait a minute, you are marrying THE Mitchell Simmons? He's one of the best agents in the country. Congrats to you! My guy runs the local BMW dealership in town, along with the Starbucks."

Kat's eyes lit up. "Thank you! So, he's the one responsible for bringing Starbucks to our town."

Candace nodded. "He is. He's from Seattle. Home of Starbucks. I met him at a convention there. After a few months of one of us going back and forth from Seattle to Georgia, he told me he wouldn't live in Sweetbriar without there being a Starbucks. So, what does he do? He got himself a franchise."

"That's what I call a commitment," Kat said.

"Right? I wasn't about to move to Seattle. Too rainy for my taste. Anyhow, let's get back to you. I got your message about this house."

"Well, thanks for meeting me. I understand that you represent the Mulderry family?"

Candace nodded. "I do. They have been looking for a buyer for a long time."

"I'm surprised they don't have a lot of offers. I've always liked this house."

"Well, Mrs. Mulderry kept the home in pretty good shape overall. As her health declined, it became harder and harder for her to keep up. So, it could use a little TLC," Candace admitted

The two ladies walked around the property.

The grass was overgrown, the house needed some paint, trees needed to be trimmed. They got up to the front covered porch. Candace took out the keys and she opened the door.

The house was still beautiful but dated. As Candace showed her around, Kat was thinking how she would tear down a wall or what color paint she would use for the living room. Her mind was racing. The family room had a beautiful fireplace, even though they were in the South, and the gourmet kitchen just needed some new countertops and new appliances. They went upstairs, there were four bedrooms. The main bedroom had a fireplace, a huge en suite that needed an upgraded tub and shower. But what won her over was the walk-in closet. It took her breath away.

"I had no idea that Mrs. Mulderry had a walk-in closet like this," Kat told Candace.

Candace said, "She was well off. But you wouldn't know it from the way she dressed when we saw her."

Kat laughed. "Those overalls and Crocs. I swear she had a different pair of Crocs for every day of the week."

Candace chuckled. "I think she did. But she was a lot of fun. "

"She was. This is a closet for a movie star."

"Well, you know she was in TV, back in the day," Candace said.

"I had heard that. She and Mr. Mulderry lived quite the life before they came to Sweetbriar."

"I bet you Mae has some stories about them. They'd be a great subject for Founders' Day for Ian to write about," Candace said

"Yeah, they would be. I can tell him. Or maybe, I'll do it since I'll be here for a bit," Kat told her.

"How long?" Candace asked. Her eyes twinkled with delight.

"Not really sure yet. Going to be helping out until Dad gets better. I didn't want to stay at home, so why not look at places to live."

Candace smiled. "They didn't want to sell it to just anyone. I bet her kids would sell to you. The price is pretty decent."

"You know how I feel about this place. I'll take it," she said. "Whatever they are offering, I'll take it. "

"Did you want to look at the gardens and the pool?"

"I'm sure they need work, but it's nothing that can't be fixed."

"Great! I'll go back and tell her kids that you'd like to put an offer in."

Kat smiled. "While you're doing that, I'll go in the back and look at the gardens and pool."

"Perfect. I'll meet you out front." Candace said as she took out her phone from her purse.

Kat went downstairs and out to the back. The gardens were a bit overgrown. The in-ground swimming pool needed a new liner and updated stones. Everything was like she remembered it. Having this home would be a dream. It overlooked the bay; it was quiet and beautiful.

As she walked around toward the front of the house, Candace was waiting for her.

"I just got off the phone with Mrs. Mulderry's son."

"And?"

"They look forward to hearing your offer," Candace said with a huge grin on her face.

Kat squealed and hugged her friend.

"I'll talk to my accountant in the city and we'll get back to you as soon as possible."

"Wonderful!" Candace said.

"This house has great bones. This is the first time since being back that I feel like I'm home," Kat noted

"Welcome Home, Kat," Candace said.

Chapter 14

After looking at the Mulderry Farmhouse, Kat decided to go back to *The Post*. She was still trying to figure out exactly what they needed to do. As she drove into *The Post's* parking lot, there stood Ross in front of a rented car.

Kat got out of the car with her purse, keys, and tote bag.

"Hello, Katherine," Ross greeted in his distinguished British accent.

It was a warm day in Sweetbriar. He wore a pair of khakis and a light blue shirt. It was early afternoon and he was already sweating profusely through his shirt, wiping the sweat off of his forehead with a handkerchief.

"Hello, Boss." Kat smiled.

"Not this time," Ross corrected. "I'm at 'your' service. I have a bunch of time to take off and I told you that I'd come down to help."

"Yes, you did. But I didn't think you were serious," Kat said.

"Why wouldn't I be? Your dad is sick, he has one of the most successful newspapers in the country, and you need help. And like I said, I have a ton of time to take off. The *Empire Post* right now can run itself. "

"I'm surprised you aren't on a beach somewhere reading a book," Kat told him.

"And what would be the fun in that?" he asked her. "I'd love it for a couple of days, and then I'd go stir-crazy. Getting that 'story' is my fix. It's like a drug."

"Well, I could use the help around here. We have a special Founders' Day edition to run. Advertising meetings, meanwhile, I have a guy developing a mobile app for phones and tablets."

"You're off to a good start," he told her. "I started a business page on Friendsbook also."

"That a girl," Ross praised. "Oh, by the way, I loved your story with Jacques Primeau. Great stuff, as usual."

"He's a really nice guy. He actually asked me a lot about dad and my grandmother."

"Civil rights icons," he said.

"That they are," Kat agreed as the two of them walked toward the door.

"We're going to need to look at some of the writers. There are some that could either use a refresher or we're going to have to lose them," Kat said.

"Oh?" Ross replied.

Kat nodded. "This is where you come in. WE should freshen up the deadline schedules. Some of the writers aren't pulling their full weight. Don't get me wrong, they are all great reporters. But while some are churning out story after story. We'll be lucky to get from others, two or three stories every three months."

"That's not good."

"Nope," she told him.

"We'll get them all on a schedule. Especially now that you'll have an online presence. The ones who aren't doing anything could be doing an exclusive article online. That could be under the newspaper's paywall. "

"Paywall?" Kat asked.

"They'll have to subscribe or be charged money to read it," Ross shared with a mischievous grin.

"Oh, I like," she said.

"The *Empire Post* does that. You wouldn't know that because you're not in administration, but that's how it works."

Kat nodded.

She showed him around *The Post*. The prestigious paper was smaller than the *Empire Post*, but held its own. People were busy working on tomorrow's issue as well as upcoming issues.

As they walked into advertising, Kat showed him that there were only a couple of people in the department.

"There's only two people in the whole advertising department?" he asked

"Yes," she said.

"I was hoping the others were at lunch," Ross commented. "You're going to need some more help in order to secure the ads, dear."

"I know. There also is no advertising schedule," Kat said.

Ross raised his eyebrows. "What?" he asked.

"Nope. We have Founders' Day, the Harvest Festival, along with Thanksgiving and Christmas, and there is no advertising schedule. "

"We'll fix that," Ross assured. "Is there anything else that I should be warned about?

"Well, my ex is back home," she told him.

"Jayson's here? Like NHL superstar Jayson McQuayde?"

Kat nodded. "He is."

"Why?"

"He apparently is injured," she informed him.

Ross's eyes narrowed. "Hmm."

"Hmm?" she asked.

"Can he write?" Ross asked.

"I have no idea. Why?" Kat asked.

"He could be the one that helps bring in advertisers and subscribers."

"How?"

"A column. Give him a column and a podcast."

Kat was stunned. She had no idea what Ross was talking about. "Why would I give him a column and a podcast?" she asked.

"Because he's a superstar athlete. He can bring national attention. And if he can do that, that will bring in advertisers and subscribers."

"I don't even know if he can write anything. I don't know about this, Ross," Kat told him.

"What is there to know, Kat? It's a no-brainer. If he needs help, help him. Just get him here and see if he'll do it."

"I would if I were on speaking terms with him," she said.

"Well, get on speaking terms with him. Your family's newspaper and legacy depend on it," Ross told her.

"It's not that simple."

"It is that simple. You go up to him, bat those pretty eyes, and talk it out with him."

She had a knot in her stomach. She knew that Ross was right. Her parents were also right, so was Thea. She had to talk to him. Maybe, after they worked things out, he would at least consider writing a column for the paper.

"I'll go talk to him. Who knows? Maybe we'll finally avoid killing each other," she quipped.

"Never know. If I can help you with talking to him, let me know," Ross offered.

"Will do," Kat said. "Welcome to Sweetbriar, Ross."

"I think I'm going to like it here," he replied.

Kat smiled wide. She was happy to see a familiar face from the city.

Chapter 15

After Kat left *The Post,* she decided to meet up with Thea at The Hat Trick for a late lunch. She would have to go to visit her father afterward and go back to the newspaper.

She walked into the diner and sat down at the booth. She could feel the tension in her shoulders. What if she saw him again? What if she couldn't control her anger? Everyone was right. It had been a long time since this all happened. She had a great career in New York, a great penthouse, a fabulous fiancé, and hopefully a new second home here where she could come when she needed a break from everything. To hold all of this anger for something was draining.

"Hey you!" Thea said as she walked into the diner and sat across from her best friend.

"Hey, thanks for meeting me. Did I pull you away from something big?" Kat asked

Thea nodded. "I need a break. I'm designing Esther Reilly's wedding gown and that woman is all over the place."

Kat looked surprised. "Oh, please tell. I need a good gossipy distraction."

"Well, Esther is so sweet. But, as you know, she's on the curvy side. We went over her initial design and it was beautiful. She was in love with it, her mom, her bridesmaids, all loved it. So we started doing the alterations and everything up to this week was going great, until she decides that the dress is bad luck because her fiancé saw her in it as she was trying it out. So, now, she wants to scrap it and wants me to design a brand-new dress with a week before her wedding."

Kat's eyes widened. "You have got to be kidding. "

"I wish I were. I tried to talk her into keeping the dress since we have been working on it for months, but nope. I could cry. Every design I have given her, she doesn't like. I already told Jake that he'll barely see me for a few days."

Kat looked sadly at her friend." That sucks. I'm sorry, Thea."

Thea shrugged. "It is what it is. People around here gotta keep me on my toes. I have some prom dresses to do after Esther's wedding so those will be fun."

Kat chuckled. "Aww, prom! How fun. I wouldn't know what it was like to go because a certain man got himself suspended just before senior prom. "

Thea laughed. "That's right. Trying to remember what he did. Was it putting Principal Harris's car on top of the high school roof?"

"Yes! And then mooning the man! All because he wouldn't let him play baseball for one game."

Thea laughed. "I remember that. Still can't believe that."

"And we got detention for laughing at it. I mean, did Harris think I was going to go against my boyfriend. I agreed with Jayson! He should have been allowed to play. That coach was such an ass."

"I know, right? I heard after we graduated that they fired the coach. Apparently, they caught him screwing Harris's wife in the gym."

Kat's mouth dropped open. "No! Why didn't I hear about this?"

"Probably too busy trying to follow Jay to Georgia State."

Kat took a deep breath. "Which brings me to why I asked you here."

Thea's eyes narrowed. "Okay..."

"Things with *The Sweetbriar Post* are a little crazy right now. It looks like I'll be here for a bit. There's hardly any ad revenue coming in and subscriptions are dropping. My boss from New York is here helping me fix the issues which can be fixed. But Ross thinks we need that special person to help attract advertisers and subscribers."

"Who?" asked Thea.

Kat took a deep breath before she replied, "Jayson. He wants to see if Jayson would be interested in doing a column and a podcast. Kind of like being like the voice of *The Post*."

Thea grinned widely. "That's fantastic! He'd be perfect for it. He'll be home all summer since the season is nearly over and due to his knee injury. You should ask him."

Kat nodded. "I should, but I don't know where to start. I swear getting mad at him is like second nature. I don't want to, but I can't help it, Thea."

"Then tell him how you feel," Thea told her. "Let it all out. You feel rage because you didn't talk about it. It's been festering inside you for eons."

"Part of me wants you to ask him for me. But, you can't."

"You are a big girl and can do this yourself," teased Thea.

"I know, I can. I'm just nervous. I haven't been this nervous since we were kids. I mean, what if he says no? Or, what if he tells me to F-off? I mean, I was a jerk to him a few days ago."

"You were. You acted like you were five with all that screaming. I had a headache," Thea told her in her Southern drawl.

"I apologize for that. All of you are right. Mom and Dad told me that I should talk to him too."

"For what it's worth, Jake and I told Jay to talk to you also. It's been too long. We are all friends. This can be worked out. We missed a bunch of time with you because of this."

"Well, you'll see me now. I'm putting in an offer on the Mulderry Farmhouse on the bay."

Thea's eyes lit up. "Kat! Are you serious! That's awesome!"

"Yes, you'll see me more. I'll be going back and forth from New York, but the house will be a great vacation home and I'll be here during holidays. The house needs some updating and some paint, but otherwise it looks great. Candace Stafford showed it to me."

"Aww, Candace!" replied Thea. "She's so sweet. Ever see that rock her husband put on her finger? It's huge."

Kat nodded. "She showed it to me. I guess her husband owns a dealership and the Starbucks here in town?"

"Bless him. One thing I missed after graduating fashion school in Los Angeles was Starbucks. And In-and-Out," Thea replied.

"I forgot about that place. Those fries!" said Kat as she rubbed her stomach. "Speaking of which, let's grab some sweet potato fries."

"Amen to that," replied Thea.

A huge shadow came over them in the middle of the table.

"What can I get you ladies?" a male voice said.

The two ladies looked up and there stood Jayson with a huge smile on his face.

Chapter 16

Thea looked at Jayson. She gave him a huge smile and a wink. Kat was frozen. It took everything in her to force a smile.

You can do it, she told herself. *You can do this.*

"Hi, Jayson," Kat said. "I just want to apologize for the other day. I wasn't expecting to see you and between that and what's going on with my dad—"

Jayson interrupted her, "It's fine. I tend to shock people wherever I go these days."

Kat chuckled.

He looked amazing. He wore a gray short-sleeved shirt and blue jeans. His hazel eyes twinkled with just a hint of mischievous intent.

"I am starving. I'll have a cheeseburger with some loaded sweet potato fries," Thea said.

"I'll have the same. The sweet potato fries are amazing. You guys did a great job with this place," Kat told him.

Jayson was in shock. "Oh my God, would you look at that. A compliment. Haven't had one of those from her in how long?" He turned to Thea.

"Seven or eight years," replied Thea.

Jayson teased, "That's it! What's the catch, Kit Kat?"

Kat laughed nervously. "Catch? There is no catch? What do you mean there's a catch? I complimented you on having a nice place, and I apologized for being a witch to you the other day. Why does there need to be a catch?"

Thea looked at her watch. "I'm going to call my assistant at the shop and let her know I'm here. I'll be right back," she told them as she got up.

Jayson sat down across from Kat in Thea's place.

"Um, our food?" Kat told him.

Jayson suddenly got serious. "It can wait for a few. What's going on?"

"Nothing," she told him

Jayson gave her a skeptical glare. "I don't believe you. Spill it."

Kat was nervous. "It's everything with my dad, that's all. The paper is having some cash flow issues. But it isn't anything we can't handle. I've been stressed about it."

Jayson nodded his head and pursed his lips. He knew her better than anyone. She wasn't telling him everything. "You sure that's all that's bugging you?" he asked.

Kat suddenly got quiet. She wrapped her hair around her ears. "No," she said.

"I am really sorry, Jay, for the other day. It's been years and it still hurts. We were going to be a team. It was you and me against the world. "

Jayson looked down at the table. "I know. I messed up. If I could take it back, I would. But look at how you turned out. You're on TV, you have a great job in New York. I've seen you a couple of times at some film premieres."

Kat looked at him in horror. "Oh God, you saw me that night at the film premiere?"

Jayson nodded. "I did. By the time I was going to talk to you, you and your date were gone."

"The minute I saw you, I left. It was too hard. If I had talked to you that night, it would have been a disaster. I was so angry. I couldn't believe, as I saw it back then, you had the gall to show up at a premiere."

"Hockey players like movies too," he quipped.

Kat chuckled. "I know you do. I guess I wasn't prepared then or the other day. Listen, I'm going to be around here for a few months until

Dad feels better. I don't want any more awkwardness or fighting," she explained.

'I'm for that. What happened is what happened. We can't change that. But we can move forward and become friends again. I miss you. I miss all four of us hanging out. We had the BEST times," Jayson said.

"We did. Thea and I were talking about the time you put Principal Harris's car on the roof at the high school."

Jayson laughed out loud. "That was a classic. Then Harris pissed me off and I mooned him and got suspended. You were so mad because I couldn't go to prom."

Kat laughed. "I was livid. Thea and her mom had made my dress and it was a small fortune. I worked a ton of weekends at *The Post* saving up for that prom, only for you to mess it up." She laughed.

"It was funny. You have to admit."

"It was hysterical. Thea and I wound up getting detention anyway, so it all worked out."

Jayson snickered. "We all wound up hanging out at the bay anyway during prom. Skinny-dip!"

"Of course you loved that," Kat teased.

"Always. You have a hot bod. Just sayin'," he told her with a wink.

"If you weren't such a jerk, I would tell you that you aren't so bad yourself. But I don't want you to get a swelled head or anything."

"Who me?" He pointed at himself.

"Always you." She smiled. "There is something that I need to ask you. And it's fine if you say no. I would understand if you didn't want to do it."

"Okay," he said.

"My boss is here from the *Empire Post* helping me out with some of the things we need to do to turn the paper around. He wondered if you would like to help with that. You're popular, talented. People are drawn to you. We think it'd be great for you to have a column and a podcast. Kinda be the voice of Sweetbriar," Kat said.

"I don't know, Kat. I'm not a great writer," he told her.

"Well, we can help you with that. You'd write what you know. If that's hockey, then it's hockey. If it's something else, then that's okay too. You do have a wonderful personality. You're witty and fun. You can talk about the current events and not piss anyone off."

Jayson was surprised. "I wasn't expecting this. You really think I could do this?"

Kat nodded. "I do. I'll give you some time to think it over," she told him.

Jayson got up from the table and nodded his head. "Let me grab your food," he said as Thea walked back in.

"How did everything go?" she asked.

"Okay. There will be no more wars. At least on my end," Kat explained.

"Did you ask him about the job at *The Post*?" Thea asked.

"He needs to think about it. I threw a lot at him."

"So, the waiting game begins?"

"It does," Kat told her friend.

Chapter 17

LATER ON THAT NIGHT, Jayson was in the apartment he shared with Ian. He was staring at the TV. Not really watching it, just staring at it. Finally, he had a decent conversation with Kat that didn't end in bloodshed or something burning down. It felt good for them to talk, even if he didn't tell her that he didn't actually sleep with Nicole that day.

His knee began to ache. He had forgotten that he was standing up at the diner for most of the day. Something he wasn't supposed to do. Jacob was out of town getting new supplies for the diner, and someone had to be there for the day-to-day operations. He walked into the kitchen and headed toward the freezer and took out an icepack. He opened the other side of the fridge and took out a bottle of beer.

By the time he wandered back on the couch, he was limping. He put his leg on the couch and pulled up his pant leg. His knee was swollen and had a huge scar that went vertically over his kneecap.

The ACL tear to his knee was no one's fault. It was a simple block into the wall. A move that happened to everyone all the time and in every game. He knew the minute he landed wrong and heard a pop that something was off. Prior to that, he was having a great season. He was already at forty-three goals and twenty-five assists. His goal was to beat his old friend from the Penguins, Sidney Crosby's goal of fifty-five so far.

He put the icepack on his knee, which was now throbbing.

Suddenly, the front door opened wide. "Honey, I'm home," Ian yelled.

Jayson took a deep breath. All the peace and quiet he had was shattered.

"Hello," he greeted his older brother. Ian took off his jacket and threw it down on the couch and slammed the door behind him.

'How was your day?" he asked as he bolted past Jayson and toward the kitchen.

"It was all right. I went to the diner and helped out most of the day. Jake had to go and grab some office supplies out of town."

Ian came back in with a bottle of beer. "How is your knee holding up?" he asked, pointing at his knee.

"It was doing fine until a few minutes ago. Nothing that a little ice and rest won't fix."

"How long are you out again?"

Jayson took a huge sip of his beer and put it down. "The rest of the season. Probably won't be back until November or December, to be honest."

"That sucks. But, selfishly, I'm happy that you're home. It's good to see you."

Jayson smiled. "Good to be home. I miss all of you a ton when I'm gone. I needed a break. My body felt like it had been through a war."

Ian took a sip of his beer and sat down next to his brother. "Well, bro, you aren't a spring chicken anymore. Those hits are starting to hurt."

Jayson nodded. "You aren't lying. Even though I have a year left on my contract, I've been thinking of slowing down lately. Figuring out my next step."

Ian took a long gulp of his beer. "Oh, what are you thinking of doing?"

"I could do what Dad does and be an analyst."

"You also have the diner," Ian reminded.

"We could expand The Hat Trick into other locations. There's a couple of spots in Atlanta and Savannah that would be perfect."

Ian smiled. "I'm game."

"But what do I do every day?" Jayson said. "Jake has the day-to-day of the diner down to a science. If you and I weren't here, he has others that he's trained to run things in case he's out."

"So that leaves?" Ian shrugged

"Working for *The Sweetbriar Post*. Kat offered me a job writing and doing a podcast."

Ian's eyes twinkled with delight. "That's fantastic! You'd be great. You have stories to tell. Go for it."

"I can't write worth anything, Ian."

"Sure you can. Write what you know. Hell, I can't believe you talked to Kat."

"You and me both. It was actually a decent conversation. No blood was shed, or furniture destroyed. She apologized for the other day."

"See, now that she knows what happened you probably feel better," Ian told him.

"Um, she doesn't know about that."

Ian rolled his eyes. "What! Are you serious? Why didn't you tell her?"

"Because, it was so long ago. We agreed just to kind of keep it moving and just be friendly and not so awkward for everyone."

Ian shook his head. "This is going to go so bad."

Jayson took another sip of his beer. "How?"

"It's just a bad feeling I have," Ian said.

"Don't poke the bear on this, Ian. Let it go."

Hey it's not me not being honest."

"What am I not being honest about? I just decided not to tell her something that doesn't matter in the whole scheme of things anymore. She's a different person than she was back then. She's who she should be. Strong, talented, gorgeous, and she's got a load of money."

Ian took a deep breath and shook his head. "This is going to go down in flames. I'm telling you. Hopefully, I'll be out of the crossfire when it happens. Did you give her an answer about working at *The Post*?"

"I told her that I would think about it," Jayson told him.

"Well, it's a good thing to be honest. You'd be great and you being there would help out the paper too...and her."

"Decisions, decisions, brother," Jayson said.

"You'll make the right one. Whatever, it may be. And if you do decide to work at *The Post* with us, please give me ample warning so that I can get an assignment somewhere out of town," Ian teased.

"Never."

"You're the worst," Ian quipped.

"Someone has to be," Jayson teased.

Chapter 18

Kat was at *The Post* working. She was in her father's office editing her story on Jacques Primeau for the *Empire Post*. She had gone to see her father earlier. Thankfully, he was improving more and more each day. As she looked over the story once more, she couldn't help but feel distracted over what happened with her and Jayson earlier.

She felt a sense of relief by talking with him. The anger was gone. She was about to press send on her story when her phone rang.

"Hello?" she said.

"Hey, babe, it's me," Mitchell greeted her on the other end. "I didn't hear from you for a couple of days and I wanted to check up on you."

"Hi, things are going okay. Dad is feeling better. They're going to release him in a few days. While he's recuperating, I'm helping out with *The Sweetbriar Post*."

Mitchell was silent for a few seconds. "Oh, how long will you be there?"

"Well, from what things are looking like, a few months. I'm taking a leave from the *Empire Post* for a bit until he's better."

"Um, hon. I love that you want to help your father, but doesn't he have people to do this for him?" Mitchell asked.

"He does. But I know the ins and outs of my family's business. We are having a little bit of a cash flow issue here. We do have a strong plan to fix it, but it's going to take some time," she explained.

"What about our wedding?" he asked

Kat couldn't believe what she was hearing. "What about our wedding? I can't really think about that now. My father nearly died from a massive heart attack and our family's newspaper is having issues."

She could hear Mitchell sigh. "You're right. I'm sorry. It was insensitive of me."

"It's okay. Everyone has a lot on their plate," she told him.

"By the way, I have not one, not two, but three homes under contract!" he said cheerfully.

Kat smiled weakly. She was tired and wanted to send this story and then go home to bed. "That's great, honey. Listen, I'll call you tomorrow. I'm going to send off this Jacques Primeau story that I've been working on and go to bed. It's getting late and I'm exhausted. It's been a long day."

"Okay, love. We'll talk tomorrow. I love you," Mitchell said.

"Love you too," she replied to him and hung up the phone.

She heard a knock at the door and looked up. She was surprised to see that it was Jayson. "Can I come in?" he asked.

Kat smiled. "Sure, come on in."

Jayson walked in and had a noticeable limp. "Are you okay?" Kat asked.

"Yes, I overdid it today. It's just sore," he explained.

Kat got up and moved a chair from the corner to across from her desk. Jayson sat down and she went back to the desk.

"If I am here too late, I can always come back tomorrow," Jayson offered.

"You're fine. I was just on the phone with my boyfriend," she told him.

"Boyfriend?"

"Yes, his name is Mitchell Simmons. He's a real estate agent."

"I've heard of him. He sold a few houses to a couple of my teammates."

"Oh nice," she replied.

"How long have you been seeing him?"

She felt awkward at the questions. She nervously tugged at her hair with her left hand. "Um, about three years." she told him. The ring sparkled from her ring finger.

Jayson grabbed her hand and raised his eyes. "He's more than your boyfriend."

Kat nodded. "This is true. He's, my fiancé. Mitchell proposed to me just before I left the city. We don't even have a date or any plans. I literally got the ring and got on a plane."

Jayson's eyes filled with sadness. "Oh. Does anyone else know?"

"I think the only person who knows is Candace Brighton and Thea. She's helping me buy the Mulderry Farmhouse."

"You're thinking of buying it?" he asked.

"Yes, I'll be here for a few months. And I thought, I miss home, and I don't want to impose on my parents. So, why not get my own place."

"God that house is beautiful. We used to pick blueberries and strawberries there every summer."

Kat laughed. "We did. She was a nice lady. I guess I'll know if her kids liked the offer in a couple of days."

Jayson nodded.

"So, what brings you here? It's late."

Jayson was nervous. He got up and began to pace. His limp was getting slightly better.

"I've been thinking about the offer you made. I'd like to do it. I don't know what I want to do yet. But I'd like to try."

Kat grinned from ear to ear. "Yes! That's awesome. We'll figure it out."

"I don't even think I can write anything. Remember me and essays and papers in school?"

"Yeah, if I remember correctly, they were pretty damn good," Kat reminded him.

"You think? Writing always used to give me such anxiety," he admitted to her.

"Write what you know. If you do that, you won't be so anxious. "

"Ian said the same thing."

"He's right. You love hockey, right? You can write about that. I don't know if you still love fishing, but you can do something about that."

"Didn't even think of that. I haven't picked up a fishing pole in a couple of years."

"You can talk about how it feels to be one with nature. The calmness of the water. How it feels when you get that tug on your line when a fish bites. Interview others who love it, same thing with hockey. It's about sharing stories about the things people care about," Kat said.

Jayson was flabbergasted. He never thought of writing in the way she described it. He was in.

"Okay, let's do this. But on one condition," he told her.

"Condition?" she asked with curiosity.

"We go fishing tomorrow. You and Me. Just a couple of friends hanging out."

Kat looked at him with hesitation.

"I don't bite, Kat. In fact, a long time ago, you liked hanging out with me."

Kat nodded. "Okay. It's a good way to rebuild our friendship and talk about what you want to do for the paper."

Jayson smiled. "That a girl. I'll pick you up at 7 a.m."

Kat raised her eyebrows. "Seven? God, that's so early."

"That's when they start to bite. Besides, if we go out there any later, it'll be too hot."

Kat nodded. "True."

"So, do we have a deal?" he asked.

"Deal," she told him.

Chapter 19

It was early the next morning. Kat tossed and turned all night. Every time she tried to close her eyes; she saw Jayson's face. As happy as she was that the two of them were now cordial, she couldn't help but wonder why he asked her to go fishing with him. Yes, they were now friends, but what brought that on?

She looked out the window, the early morning sun poked through her childhood bedroom window.

She turned and glanced at the clock. It was 6 a.m. If she showered and dressed, she could get to the bay in the nick of time.

If she didn't show up, then what would that say? She'd probably lose Jayson as a way to help the paper and her family. Also, it would probably start World War III.

She hated to do this, but she picked up the phone from her nightstand and called Thea.

"It's 6 a.m., Kat. This better be good," Thea told her groggily.

"I'm sorry to wake you. I need some advice. Listen, Jayson came by *The Post* last night—"

"And?" Thea interrupted.

"He told me that he wants to help."

Thea, sounding exhausted, replied, "That's great. Why do you need my advice on that?"

"It's not that," Kat explained. "He wants me to go fishing with him today."

"What?" Thea asked.

"That's what I said. What do I do?"

"What's the big deal? We all used to go fishing together all the time."

"I know we did, but Thea, we were together then. We all were friends then. He and I are okay now, but I still feel a little awkward. I haven't spent time with him in seven years."

Thea chuckled. "It's no different than spending time with him back then. He's harmless."

"I just feel weird. It's the first time hanging with him in a bit. If I don't go, he probably won't write for us. If I go..."

"Then everything will be okay, Kat," Thea told her.

Kat took a deep breath. She didn't know why she felt so nervous. "You're right. It'll be fine. What can go wrong? It's Jayson. He's funny, smart."

"And he is your ex," Thea reminded her.

"And he's my ex."

"Let me shower and get dressed. I'll drag Jake out of bed and meet you at the docks in thirty minutes," Thea told her.

Kat was relieved. "Thank you! I owe you big time."

"You sure as hell do. I was up all night working on that dress. She finally loved a design I made."

"Oh, wow. That's good though."

"I can't wait until this wedding is over on Saturday. I'm going to be doing alterations literally every single day until then. I could use a couple of hours off anyway. I'll see you there," Thea confirmed to her as she hung up.

Kat sat on the side of the bed. She put her phone down and raked her hand through her long hair. Since that was settled, she wondered what she should wear. She got up and went through her drawers. She found a pair of old jean shorts and a blue T-shirt. She grabbed them and put them on the foot of her bed.

After a quick shower, she put her hair in a ponytail and got dressed.

By the time she got to the docks, Thea was there dressed in sunglasses, shorts, and a halter. She met Kat with a huge paper bag. Jacob followed slowly behind her.

"Thanks for meeting me," Kat said.

Thea hugged her. "We bring reinforcements. There's coffee and breakfast burritos for everyone."

Kat waved at Jacob who was behind Thea. "Hey, Jake."

Jacob, who was in jeans in a black T-shirt, smiled warmly and waved.

"You look exhausted," Kat said to her friend.

"After this, Jake and I are taking a long nap. It's going to be a hot one today."

The three walked toward the dock where they saw the boat, *All In*. It was a phrase that not only Jayson used to say to Kat, but Jayson and Jacob's father used on television a great deal.

It was a nice boat. It was white with blue trim. The McQuaydes had owned it for a few years. The four of them spent a lot of time on the boat. Kat was happy that they still had it.

Standing in front of the boat was Jayson. He looked refreshed and happy wearing a pair of khakis and a white shirt. His eyes filled with surprise as he saw three people.

"Hi," he said to everyone.

Kat smiled widely. "Hey, good morning! I was talking with Thea and I told her that we were going fishing today."

"And I said to her, that's great! The four of us haven't done anything together in years. So, now that everyone is getting along, why don't we get the band back together?" Thea chimed in, giving Jayson a cheeky grin.

Jayson chuckled. He pointed at the bag. "Cool. What's in the bag?"

Jacob yawned. He put on his sunglasses in an attempt to hide his exhaustion. "Coffee and breakfast burritos from the diner," he replied.

"Awesome. I didn't get a chance to eat anything. Ian was in the kitchen with all of his juicing crap, yakking away, and I'm not even dealing with that."

"Dear God, it's too early for that," Jacob told him.

"That's what I said," Jayson agreed. "He had everything all out, I couldn't eat anything out of the fridge if I tried. I swear everything we had in the fridge was on the counter. So, thanks for this."

"Let's get going before it gets too hot and no fish bite," Jacob said.

Jayson nodded and the four of them got on the boat.

Jayson took Jacob aside and whispered, "What the hell?"

Jacob was equally perplexed. He continued to yawn. "Your guess is as good as mine. Thea woke me up and told me that we needed to go fishing this morning. I didn't get back into town until 1 a.m."

Jayson looked surprised. "Oh!"

"I am clueless, Jay. I just want to sleep."

"I finally talked to Kat yesterday, and I thought we worked things out," Jayson explained to his brother.

"I think so. I don't see food or coffee going everywhere so I'm seeing that as a good sign," teased Jacob.

"Ha ha."

Chapter 20

Jacob turned to his brother on the boat and smiled. He was relieved that Jayson and Kat were talking. Thea and Kat were at the front of the boat. "I'm so glad you finally told her about what happened because, man, that went on too damn long," Jacob told him.

Jayson's eyes narrowed. He looked around to make sure Kat wasn't near them and said in a low voice, "I didn't tell her."

"What do you mean you didn't tell her, Jay? The heck?"

"I figured why bother? It's been years. She's engaged anyway, so why does it matter?"

Jacob's eyes filled with surprise. "Engaged? What are you talking about?"

Jayson shook his head. "When you get a chance, look at her left hand. She's got an enormous rock on it. I'm surprised no one else caught it."

"Not surprised you did. It must be that ex radar."

"I would think Thea knows. I'm surprised she didn't say anything to me."

"Well, maybe she thought it was better that it came from Kat. How are you feeling about it?"

Jayson's face looked strained. He was confused.

"I'm happy for her. I really am. But, there's just a little part of me that wonders, what if things were different?"

"Well, you made that choice for her. Look at her career," Jacob pointed out to him. "I mean look at her. She's rich and successful."

"And if she had stayed home, she would have been a wife and mom with a dream," Jayson reminded him. "I'd make that decision again."

They both looked over at Kat and Thea, who were laughing and waving at the two of them. "You better either tell her the truth, Jayson, or pray she never finds out. Because if she does, she's going to tear you up. And you'll deserve it. I'm not backing you up this time," Jacob warned him.

"She won't find out," Jayson replied.

Jacob began to walk over to the girls. He shook his head.

"Thanks so much for coming. I owe you big time," she told Thea again.

"Don't worry about it. It's what friends do. You'd do it for me."

Kat nodded. "I totally would. You know that."

Jacob wandered over to them and picked up Kat's left hand. "Oh, would you look at this," he announced to everyone as Kat's ring shown brilliantly in the early morning sun.

"This thing?" Kat quipped. "I got that from my guy just before I left the city."

Jacob took a look at the ring. He was impressed. "It's nice. Congrats."

"Thank you, Jake. When are you going to put a ring on my bestie?" Kat asked.

Jacob's eyes widened with surprise. "Um."

Thea interrupted. "Oh, he was NOT ready for that," she told Kat as she watched him squirm, with a smile "Ten years. Reminding you."

"Has it been ten? God, it feels like it was yesterday," he said with a wide grin.

"Clock is ticking, babe," Thea told him, giving him a peck on the cheek.

Jayson chuckled. "I'm already on it."

Thea's eyes raised.

"Didn't think I was, huh? I want to live to see the next twenty to thirty years," he teased.

"What's everyone talking about?" Jayson asked.

"Valuing life," Kat joked.

"Oh?" Jayson said.

"I got reminded that Thea and I have been together ten years and that I need to put a ring on it soon."

"I see. In other words, you're getting schooled," Jayson quipped.

Jacob shook his head. "Not you too?"

"Well, Thea is like a little sister to me. And our families are tight. And I know you love her so..."

"Tell 'em, Jay," Kat chimed in, giving Jayson a wink.

"I got you, Thea," Jayson told Thea.

"Glad you do," Thea said to him.

Jacob felt surrounded. "I'm working on it, okay?" He turned to Thea. "I love you. I want to be with you forever. Give me a bit. I promise you. You'll have a ring. "

Thea gave him a wide smile. "I know. Our lives are crazy right now. Between the diner and the shop, an engagement never even crossed my mind. We are joking with you."

Jayson chuckled. "I have missed this with all of us."

"Same!" Thea told everyone. "We are the Four Musketeers! Period!"

"We're back!" Kat said.

Jayson couldn't help but look at Kat. She was smiling and so happy. It was like old times. He knew that despite what everyone was telling him, he definitely made the right decision.

"We are! Let's get going before the fish stop biting. I'm starving," he told everyone.

Thea opened the bag and began to give everyone a to-go cup and a burrito wrapped in aluminum foil.

"Let's go!" Kat shouted, as she took her cup of coffee and a burrito.

"You haven't lived, Kat, until you had one of Jake's breakfast burritos," Thea said.

Kat opened the foil packet. The burrito was filled with cheese, eggs, meat, and veggies.

"It looks amazing!" Kat told her.

"There's chorizo sausage, Colby Jack cheese, eggs, tomatoes, and peppers."

Kat took a bite and she was in heaven. "This is fantastic! When did you get so good at this, Jake?"

Jake shrugged. "I always loved to cook. It's relaxing to me. When hockey fell through, I went for my next favorite thing to do."

"Glad you did. The Hat Trick is a great place. Grossman's Diner was okay. But the two of you are building something special in town," Kat shared, looking over at Jayson.

"Damn, another compliment. That's three in the last twenty-four hours," Jayson quipped.

Kat chuckled. "It's true. I missed this. All of us talking. Joking. It's food for the soul."

"You have friends in the city though," Thea said.

"I do. And they're great. But it's not like the three of you. I know that I can call you guys at any time and you'd be there. Even if we are pissed at each other," Kat told them.

"I feel the same," Jacob said.

Jayson went and began to drive the boat offshore.

Kat was home now. She really was at home as she stared at the three of them. There wasn't anything they wouldn't do for each other.

Nothing.

Chapter 21

The days following the Four Musketeers fishing trip were fun and freeing for Kat. She was at *The Sweetbriar Post*. She oversaw daily editorial meetings, made sure deadlines were met, and was helping Jayson find his footing in a new space.

He opted for working in the sports department. His first column would appear in the special Founders' Day edition and be about his family's legacy in hockey.

It was fun talking with him about the love of the sport. To see his passion over something that she as a teen thought was a hobby of his turn into a career was mind-blowing for her.

Instead of her being angry with him, she turned into a fan.

There were still a few things he needed to work on, but as she read through the first draft of his column, she was proud. It was good. Very good.

She wandered over to the sports department in the newsroom and there he sat studiously looking over his notes in an empty cubicle. He was in the office a couple of days during the week and spent the rest of the time helping at the diner or at physical therapy.

"Knock. Knock," she said as she watched him stare at his computer screen.

He was thrilled to hear her voice. He turned around and smiled. "Hey, you are a welcome surprise. What's going on?"

She sat on the edge of his desk. "Not much. Everything is going well. I'm about ready to help Mom bring Dad home and wanted to check on you."

"Kat, that's great. Tell him I said hi. I'll let my dad know. He'll be in town in a few days."

Kat was thrilled. Jayson's father, Dennis, was her father's best friend. The retired NHL superstar was now a well-known sports analyst in Atlanta.

"I will! It'll be great to see your father. How does he like broadcasting?"

Jayson turned away from the computer and toward her. "He loves it. He says it's better than getting beat up on or slammed against a damn barrier."

Kat laughed. "I bet."

"He says the pay is nice too."

Kat smiled. "Yes, television pays pretty well if you can get into it. I enjoy my guest spots when I do them."

"I have to admit, I've been thinking a lot about what I'm going to do when my career is all done. Ever since you asked me to do this, I've been thinking, how much longer do I have in the tank?"

Kat shrugged. "Oh, well. You'll know when you're ready. When does your current contract end?"

"End of next year, he told her. "I don't know if I want to continue to take any more hits. The thought of it makes my body ache."

Kat looked sad. "I'm sorry, Jay. Whatever you decide, you have my support and *The Post*. Which is why I'm here to see you."

"Oh?" asked Jayson.

Kat nodded. "Yes, I just read over your first draft of your Founders' Day column."

"And?"

Kat smiled. "It's pretty good. Just some minor stuff. But I like it. You're doing a great job."

Jayson appeared relieved. "I really didn't know what I was going to write about. Since everyone told me to write what I knew. I decided to focus on my family and hockey. Two things I know a thing or two about."

"Well, it's great. Our sports editor, Morty, should be sending it back to you to fix some things and then, you'll be all set with it. Know what you want to do next?"

Jayson shrugged. "Not a clue. But my first podcast guest will be Dad."

"Nice! We'll do a subscriber tie in with that. In fact, I'm going to go to Shooter's and speak with the new owner after Dad gets settled at home."

Jayson suddenly went blank. "You know Nicole is the new owner, right?"

Kat nodded. "I know. It's okay. All of that was a long time ago."

Jayson sighed in relief. "Yes, it was. I actually haven't seen her since that day."

Kat was pleasantly surprised. "Really?"

Jayson nodded. "Really. I felt horrible. I couldn't even look at her after that. I was disgusted with myself."

"As you should have been," Kat told him. "I was a good catch."

"You were," Jayson agreed sadly. "Mitchell is lucky to have you."

"He's great. I can't wait for you to meet him. He's funny, smart."

"Loaded!" Jayson said.

Kat laughed. "That he is. He's a good real estate agent."

"Self-made man. Gotta respect that."

"As are you, Jayson. You've done well for yourself too. Any woman would be lucky to have you," Kat told him.

Jayson's face said it all. He was sad and felt enormous guilt over what happened.

"Yeah," he replied.

"Let me go to the hospital and on to Shooter's. I'll see you tomorrow?"

Jayson nodded. "Yeah. I'll be here."

Kat got up and left and headed toward her car. Her phone rang. She saw Candace's name on the caller ID. She got a lump in her throat as she answered. She hoped for great news.

"Hey, Candace!" Kat said as she opened her car door.

"Hey, Kat. How's it going?" Candace asked

"Pretty good. Things are progressing. About to head out to the hospital and bring Dad home."

"Oh, Kat! That's great! I'll make sure I stop by when he's settled. Listen, I have great news. The Mulderry kids accepted your offer. Congrats! You have a farmhouse!"

Kat squealed for joy. "Oh, Candace! Really? I got the farmhouse?"

"You did! Congrats, you are now a homeowner."

Kat was excited. She had always wanted this house. She would have a nice home away from home when she came to visit. Owning the Mulderry Farmhouse was a childhood dream. She couldn't wait to hold the keys and get started on renovations. "

"Thank you, Candace! I'll be in touch."

"Yes, I'll let you know in a few days about the inspection and close date. Congrats, sweetie. Talk to you later. We have to get Thea and do a girls' night soon!"

"Yes! Talk to you soon." Kat hung up.

Chapter 22

At the McKinnon home, Kat and the rest of the family were getting their father, Michael, settled in after his hospital stay. He was definitely looking better. While he was in the hospital, they had already begun his new low sodium, low calorie diet. Kat noticed, in the few weeks that she had been home, how thin his face was.

"Okay, Dad. Let's get you on the couch," Kat coached as she, her sisters, and Mom helped him walk toward the couch.

"Y'all are acting as if I can't walk. I can walk to my own couch," he told them as he struggled to break free from their hovering. The family's matriarch, Mae McKinnon, sat in a plush chair across from the couch. She looked over at him and shook her head.

"Son, if you don't let them take care of you, you and I will have it out. It's too hot for you to be starting nonsense."

"See, Daddy. Listen to Grandma," Kat replied to him.

After helping him get onto the couch, his wife Claire headed straight into the kitchen.

"It's so good to be home with my whole family," Michael said. "I can't wait to get back at the paper in a few days. Gotta lot of work to do."

"You will do no such thing. The doctor told you to rest," Mae scolded.

"Mom, I have to work on the Founders' Day stuff. I'm feeling better," he retorted.

Claire came back with a garbage bag and a box full of junk food.

"Mike, I would like for you to say goodbye to your little friends," she told him.

She began with three bags of potato chips, then the bag of pretzels.

Michael looked longingly at the junk food. "Really, babe?" he said to his wife.

"Bye, cheese puffs!" she said, putting three bags of cheese puffs in the garbage bag.

"This is just the beginning. Kat, did you get the stash in his office?"

Kat nodded. "It's gone, Mom."

Michael looked at his daughter with dismay. "Kat, no!"

"Yes, Daddy. Yes. The doctor says, you have to change everything. No more junk."

"I know. But a little something now and then won't hurt," he pouted.

"You can't stop. It'll start with one chip and then it's a bag, and by the end of the day, it's two bags, a sundae, a soda, and cheese fries from The Hat Trick," Mae told him.

"Jayson and Jacob are working on making a heart conscious menu. They did that with you in mind," Kat informed.

"So, you talking to Jayson now?" Michael said, raising his eyebrows.

The whole family glanced at her with a surprised look on their faces.

Kat took a deep breath. "Yes. I am. In fact, I asked Jayson to help out at the paper, he's working with us twice a week." she told everyone as she sat down next to her father.

"Dad, I took a leave of absence from the *Empire Post* to help turn things around at the paper. To help gain advertisers and subscribers, I decided on building a mobile app and began the process of putting *The Sweetbriar Post* online. We are already seeing results from online advertising by putting a few stories up on our Friendsbook page. "

Michael snickered. "You're kidding me, right?"

Kat shook her head, "No. We are doing some online promotions on the page and so far, so good."

"What's the increase?" Michael said

"Five percent," Kat told him. "It's a start and when the paper is completely online, I fully expect the advertising to double. That should happen by the end of the month."

Michael seemed skeptical. "No one is going to go on a computer or a social media site to read a paper, Kat."

"People do all the time. My popularity came from my articles going online on Friendsbook and on the *Empire Post's* site."

"We should have been online years ago," Mae added. "Subscribers are leaving because they want an option."

"What's great about being online is that our new subscribers don't just have to be in Sweetbriar. They can be nationwide. As with our new advertising partners," Kat said.

"Don't like this, Kat," Michael told her.

"Well, Dad, I don't care. We can do this my way, or Grandma's way, which is to sell the paper."

Michael looked over at his mother with fury. "I told Grandma that would kill you if she did that. So, please let me help. Jayson is a nationally known NHL superstar, he is going to be writing for us on occasion and as the voice of *The Post*, he's launching a podcast. His first guest is your best friend, Dennis McQuayde."

Michael looked at his daughter with concern. "You have enough going on with your own career instead of helping me with mine," he told her.

"I learned from the best. It's fine. The cash flow problem can be fixed. You just rest and get yourself healthy. I got this," she confirmed.

Michael nodded. Kat kissed him on the forehead and got up.

"Where are you going?" Michael asked.

"Shooter's. Going to talk to the new owner and discuss advertising with us. I'll be back. "

"You know that Nic—" Claire attempted to tell Kat and she interrupted.

"Yep. It's fine, Mom. Moving forward. It's been years."

Claire smiled. "Okay. You're my baby and I'm always going to look out for you."

"If I need reinforcements, I'll call you," Kat told her. "I love you, Mama."

"Love you, too, sweetheart."

Chapter 23

As Kat drove through town to get to Shooter's, she went through every scenario on how she would deal with Nicole.

Would I tell her to F-off? If I do that, then you can kill any potential advertising dollars for the bar goodbye, she thought.

Should I talk to her about it and then talk about advertising? Should I not say anything and feel stupid in the process? Why was it easier dealing with Jayson about this, than it was about to be for Nicole?

Nicole really wasn't really anyone she cared about.

She was pretty, but came from the wrong side of the tracks. They had all met her as they began high school. Nicole was in and out of foster homes as a kid, while her mother drank and slept with anyone who had a pulse. After one of the boyfriend's tried to push Nicole, Nicole's grandmother, who lived in Sweetbriar, took her in.

Nicole was in and out of trouble during school. From stealing cars, to being in bars. She was nothing like the rest of the kids who grew up here.

The two of them never meshed. Nicole thought of her as some rich, stuck-up snob and Kat just couldn't deal with Nicole constantly getting into trouble and bringing her boyfriend, Jayson, along for the ride at times.

She never understood the soft spot Jayson had for Nicole. Sure, Nicole was pretty with medium length, light brown hair and gray eyes, but she never saw the appeal. To her, Nicole was her own worst enemy.

Kat was surprised when Thea told her that she was going to be the new owner of Shooter's. The girl barely went to class, how would she even know how to own a bar?

Kat rolled her convertible in front of the bar and got out.

From the looks of it, the place was getting a much-needed makeover. There was updated paint up on the front of the bar, along with a new steel and neon sign on the front. As she walked in, there was a brand-new double glass door.

She looked around. The bar looked great. Updated bar, barstools, several brand-new tables. The walls were gray and trimmed in shiplap. There were construction workers busily fixing up the place as she walked around.

"Be careful, ma'am." one of the workers said to Kat.

Kat stepped over a toolbox and smiled nervously at the worker. "Excuse me? Do you know where I can find the owner?" she asked. The construction worker nodded his head while drilling a hole through a beam. "Yeah, she's in the back feeding her kid."

Kat raised her eyes with surprise. *So she has a child?* she thought.

"Thank you," she told the guy and she made her way back into the office area.

"Griffin, you have to eat this," Kat heard Nicole say.

The child screamed at the top of his lungs and said, "No!"

Kat saw Nicole from the office door. She looked exhausted. The gray eyes were now a little lined and the hair was a little darker than she remembered. Her clothes were full of sawdust and paint. Her little boy was dirty, probably from having too much fun doing DIY in the bar. He was adorable with blond hair and gray eyes like his mother.

"Griffin, please eat these for Mommy. Eat these carrots and I'll take you to The Hat Trick for an ice cream cone later. You've been such a good boy."

The little boy had to be at least two or three. He sat in a high chair, yelling at the top of his lungs. "No!" he screamed.

Nicole put her head down on the high chair tray.

Kat knocked on the door.

Nicole looked up and gave her a blank stare. "Can I help you?" she asked.

"Yes, Nicole. Remember me, I'm Kat McKinnon. We went to school together. We had a meeting today to talk about advertising for Shooter's."

"Oh, is that today?" Nicole said. She looked down at herself. She was sweaty, her hair was in a bun, and she had no makeup on. "Oh Geeze, I'm sorry, Kat. Of course, I remember who you are. How are you?" Nicole smiled weakly.

"I'm good. I'm helping out my father with the newspaper for a while and I wanted to talk to you about doing some ads for Shooter's. The place looks great," Kat told her.

"I look a mess," Nicole countered.

Kat shook her head. "You look fine. You obviously have a lot going on between the bar and this cutie," Kat said as she waved at the little boy who waved back.

"This is my little boy, Griffin." Nicole smiled as she picked him up and put him on her hip.

Kat grinned widely. "Hi, Griffin, my name is Kat. It's good to meet you," she said, shaking his little hand.

"We were trying to eat some lunch. But he obviously has other plans."

Kat snickered.

"I'll take him, Nicole," said a lady who came into the office.

"Can you bring him to Nan's and she'll put him down for a nap?" Nicole asked.

The girl nodded and walked away with the child.

"She's one of our new managers. Actually, she's my niece. Griffin loves her."

"He's sweet." Kat said.

Nicole nervously moved the high chair and some stuff off of her desk and pulled a chair from the corner to the front of her desk for Kat.

"Thanks, Kat," Nicole told her as she sat down. Nicole sat at her desk.

"So, what do you have in mind for advertising?"

"Well, I was thinking since we are doing a Founders' Day supplement, we could give you a new business rate. Usually, all the businesses are showcased. I'd like to make sure that Shooter's got a prime spot for its reopening."

Nicole's tired eyes glittered with delight. "That's fantastic!"

"The new rate isn't bad at all. If you have anything weekly that you want, like if you're having live acts. We can discuss that. Usually, the more frequently you advertise, the cheaper the rates get in your package. Especially, the first year," Kat informed her.

"I like it," Nicole said.

"How did you inherit Shooter's?" Kat asked.

"Well, after what happened with you and Jayson. I left town too for a while. I went to business school and part time, I tended bar to help pay for school. I finished school, married a drunk, divorced, and came back here and helped out at Shooter's. I tended bar, did payroll, managed the workers. I was just as surprised as anyone when Mr. Shooter left me the bar. I really wanted to do it right. So, I had some savings and I'm updating everything since it was like fifty years old."

Kat laughed. "He was a nice guy."

Nicole nodded. "Mr. Shooter was. He took me under his wing so many times when I gave up on myself. When I couldn't talk to anyone, he was there for me. He paid my way to come back home after I left my husband."

Kat felt bad. Nicole hadn't had the best time after she left town. The least she could do was clear the air with her.

"Listen, I need to apologize to you."

Nicole looked at her strangely. "For what?"

"I had judged you. I always did. You always were the one who defied everyone in school."

"But you had the guy. Man, I dug him. You were perfect. You had money, the looks, the friends, and him. You have nothing to apologize for. I was jealous of everything you had . "

"And I was jealous of how adventurous you were. Until that day," Kat said sadly.

"What a joke that was. I really thought he was into me. He loved you so much," Nicole admitted.

Kat shrugged. "I don't understand."

"He used me. He was so drunk. He was upset that you were staying here in Sweetbriar."

"Huh?" Kat looked confused.

"He had to make you leave. He hated that you wanted to stay here when you had a chance to go away to school and become something," Nicole told her.

"Who? Jayson?" Kat asked. "Listen, he and I are okay. Whatever happened was years ago. So you slept with him. It is what it is. Ya know? Don't let it bother you. Everyone does crazy things."

Nicole's eyes raised. Her mouth opened wide. "Oh my God. He didn't tell you, did he?" Nicole asked her.

"Tell me what?"

"We never slept together, Kat. He paid me to stage it. He wanted you to go to school and become something and not be stifled here. I adored him so much that I went along with it. After you saw us, he literally gave me a couple hundreds and never spoke to me again. He was heartbroken," Nicole told her.

Kat was in shock. She didn't know if she wanted to strangle Jayson or hug Nicole.

How could he do this to her? And more importantly, not tell her the truth.

Her eyes filled with tears. "I'm sorry, Nicole. I'll have Lois send over the advertising package. I think you'll like it."

Kat began to leave. Nicole tried to stop her. "Kat, I'm so sorry," she pleaded. "I really thought you knew by now. It's been such a long time."

"I didn't know. I'll deal with Jayson. Thank you for telling me, Nicole," Kat said and ran off.

Chapter 24

Kat raced out of the parking lot. She was in a rage. *How could he? Why didn't he tell her?* Was the fishing trip and all the reminiscing a lie? She was full of emotions. Back then, she would have stayed and gone to school. Georgia State was a great school. She had plans to go there and stay for him. That was a choice she was willing to make.

All in, my ass!, she thought.

She needed to talk to someone, so she pulled into Thea's boutique called Fancy, which was up the street from *The Post*.

The boutique was busy on this late spring day. Women were buying prom dresses and bridal gowns. Girls were buying trendy tops and other designer items. Thea designed a lot of the items herself. Kat was proud of her best friend and had told her several times to expand Fancy to other parts of Georgia.

She walked around the small crowd to look for Thea. She literally ran into Candace, who had a bunch of dresses and jeans in her arms.

"Hey, Candace! I'm so sorry."

Candace had dropped the items. She and Kat began to pick them up. "Oh, honey, it's no problem. I was heading to the dressing room to try these on." The two ladies looked around at the crowd. "It is a madhouse in here today," Candace observed.

"It is. I was looking for Thea," Kat said.

"Oh, she's in her office, working on that damn bridal gown. That woman should be ashamed for putting Thea and her team through that. What a mess!" Candace said.

"Thanks, honey. I'll go talk to her," Kat told her as she wandered through the back.

She found Thea and her team working on the bridal gown. The gown was placed on a mannequin, as Thea was pinning pieces of the gown together on the form.

"There you are," Kat said leaning on the door. She was distraught.

Thea looked at her friend's face with concern. "What's going on?"

"I need to talk to you for a sec," Kat told her.

Thea excused herself and the two of them went outside. "What's wrong?" Thea asked.

"Jayson never slept with Nicole. I just left Shooter's."

Thea closed her eyes and sighed. "Oh boy..."

Kat looked confused. "Don't even tell me that you knew, Thea?!"

"I told him that he should have told you—"

Kat interrupted, "What!"

"I actually thought he did after I saw the two of you finally talking."

"Why didn't you tell me?" Kat asked.

"Because it wasn't up to me. He lied; he owes it to you to tell the damn truth. I told him this was going to blow up in his face."

"I don't understand this. Why would he lie to me? Why even go through all of that if he didn't actually sleep with her?"

"Because he loved you," Thea said.

Kat rolled her eyes. "He had a funny way of showing it," Kat said as she walked away.

"Kat, I'm sorry."

Kat was too frustrated to say anything. She just got in her car and left.

She drove around for hours. She didn't understand it. He smiled in her face and acted like he did nothing. She was slowly letting him back in. God, he was now at the paper.

She was seething. *Why didn't he tell me the truth? What did I do to deserve this?* she thought.

She continued to drive in circles. She pulled into The Hat Trick. She didn't even know why.

She got out of the car and went in. She suddenly felt hungry.

"Hi, can I take your order?" the young waiter asked.

Kat looked over the menu. There was nothing really appealing. She looked up at him.

"Any specials?" she asked the young man.

"We have a great chicken Caesar salad, there's chicken à la king, and there's meatloaf."

"I'll take the chicken à la king," she told the young man as she gave him the menu.

"Anything to drink?" he asked.

"Water is fine."

The young waiter nodded and left. She glanced around the diner, thankful that she didn't see Jacob or Jayson. She needed to process everything."

After a few minutes, her food came. She looked at it for a bit before she started to play with it.

Then she heard him.

"Hey, Matt, how is everything going in here?" Jayson asked the young waiter.

"Oh hey, Jayson," the waiter greeted. "All is well.

His sweet Southern drawl was like nails on a chalkboard.

She saw red. The next thing that she remembered was picking up the chicken à la king and tapping him on the shoulder.

He turned around. "Oh hey, how did it go at Shooter's?" he asked her.

She said nothing. She poured the food all over him.

"That's how it went!" she told him. She threw some money on the table and stormed out.

She didn't look at his expression or even care. She was done. She wanted to go back to the city. Maybe being here wasn't the best thing after all. All anyone had done since she'd been home was lie to her. She felt like a fool. She didn't deserve this. Not at all. She couldn't believe that the one person who couldn't stand her was the one who told her the truth.

Chapter 25

J ayson stood in the middle of the diner in disbelief. He had a plate of food on him and he was clueless.

He looked around and noticed people staring and snickering.

Thea came in a minute later.

"Oh, I see she beat me. Crap!" she told him.

Jayson's eyes flared. "What in the hell is going on?" he asked her.

"She knows, Jayson," Thea told him.

Matt, the young waiter, had given Jayson a towel. Jayson's face turned white.

"I told you that you should have told her," Thea continued.

Jayson took a deep breath and began to wipe his face. "She'll get over this. Let her calm down," he told his old friend.

Thea was livid. She took a bowl of soup from an empty booth and poured it on him.

"Are you freakin' serious?" he yelled at her.

"Are you? She's angry. Not just at you. But at me too! You could have avoided all of this if you had just told her the damn truth. Jake and I warned you."

"Why is she mad at you? You did nothing," he yelled.

"As her best friend, I should have had her back and told her! But I didn't. I had yours though, and I shouldn't have. It was a stupid thing you did. Period. It was selfish."

"How was it selfish? She wouldn't have gone otherwise. I had to let her go or else she would have been stuck here."

"You should have let her make that decision, Jayson. You were a selfish prick. Now, thanks to you, we probably lost a friend."

"And I probably lost my job at *The Post*," he told her.

Thea hit him on the arm and stormed out as Jacob was coming in. Jacob looked at his brother covered in food and snickered.

"Kat again?" he asked his twin.

Jayson nodded. "Yeah. With a side of Thea."

Jacob shook his head. "Welp. I take it Kat found out you didn't actually sleep with Nicole?"

Jayson began to wipe himself off again. "That would be an accurate observation."

"Why is Thea mad at you?" Jacob asked.

"Sounds like she and Kat talked before Kat came in. Kat blamed her for not telling her."

Jacob shook his head in disbelief. He looked at Jayson wipe off soup and chicken à la king from his face and clothing.

"I don't want to hear the I told you so, Jake. Not today."

"Well, you are because it's true. Make it right," Jacob scolded him. "And clean yourself up. Dinner crew is going to be in here and I could use a hand."

"I was going to try and talk to Kat," Jayson told him.

"I'd give her a day or two to cool down. It's going to be busy in here and I could use a hand," Jacob explained.

"Let me wash up and change and I'll be back," Jayson replied as he walked out the door.

"You have twenty minutes," Jacob told him. Jayson stormed out. He went outside. He had hoped there was a glimpse. Just a shred of hope that Kat or Thea were in the parking lot.

"Damnit," he said to himself. He got into his car and left.

Kat was in front of the Mulderry Farmhouse. Overlooking the bay, the beach in front of the home had always been a source of comfort to her. The calm of the water, the smell of the wildflowers along the shoreline.

She sat in front of the beach overlooking the water. She didn't hear Thea come up from behind her.

"I had a feeling you were here," Thea said as she sat down next to her.

Kat gave her friend a reluctant stare and looked back at the bay.

"I'm sorry, Kat. I should have told you. You were right about that."

Kat took a deep breath and turned to Thea. Her eyes were filled with tears. "It's not even your fault. I just feel duped all over again by him. I'm just so frustrated. I don't get why he made it up and why he didn't tell me when he and I were talking a few weeks ago."

"For what it's worth, I spilled soup on him and told him what a selfish prick he was," Thea shared.

Kat began to laugh. "He can have some soup with his chicken à la king." She snickered.

Thea let out a huge laugh. "Is that what that was?" she asked.

Kat laughed. "Yeah. I don't even know why I went in there. I wasn't hungry."

"You went in there because you chose violence," Thea quipped.

"I guess. I had seen him at the paper earlier. He knew I was going to talk to Nicole. He said nothing. Just that it's in the past."

"Did he really think she wasn't going to say anything about what really happened?" Thea asked.

"Guess so. Nicole seemed sincere. She's got a kid now. "

"I heard that. She's been through a rough time the last few years. Good that she's the new owner of Shooter's," Thea said.

"Yeah. We all have made mistakes. Sorry, I prejudged her. I guess she had a thing for Jayson once upon a time too."

Thea snickered. "Who didn't back then? He was and still is hot."

Kat looked at her friend with surprise. "Well, he is," Thea continued. "When he's not doing stupid things. He's a charmer."

"That he is," agreed Kat.

"What are you going to do?" Thea asked her.

"No idea. I need a bit."

Her phone began to buzz. She picked it up and noticed it was Mitchell on the other end. "God, I am not in the mood to talk to him," Kat told her friend.

"Is that Jay?" Thea asked.

"No. It's Mitchell. "

"Oh," Thea said.

Kat looked at her left hand and at the ring. "I thought I'd be over the moon when Mr. Right proposed. Why is it that I feel more annoyance than happiness?" Kat asked her friend.

"Maybe he's not the one," Thea stated.

"I don't know. He's funny, smart, successful. We get along great."

"You never got closure with the other. When you have that, see how you feel," Thea suggested.

"Sorry, I went off on you. I love you, Thea."

Thea put her head on her friend's shoulder. "Love you too, Kit Kat. I have your back always," Thea vowed.

Chapter 26

It was a couple of days later and Jayson decided to take his chances and go into *The Post*.

He hadn't heard anything from his sports editor or Kat. *No news is good news*, he thought as he sauntered into the sports department.

His sports editor, Morty Young, was this tall, gregarious man with black hair and brown eyes. He wore a pair of khakis and a yellow short-sleeved shirt.

"Hey, Jay!" Morty greeted.

Jayson sat down at the cubicle across from Morty's desk.

"Hey, Mort, how's it going?"

"Okay, I got a message from Kat. She wants to see you in her office as soon as possible."

He closed his eyes. It was happening. He finally was getting a footing with writing this Founders' Day article and she was going to can him for staging something years ago.

"How good of a mood was she in?" Jayson asked Morty.

Morty shrugged as he took a swig of his coffee. "I don't know. She seemed okay. What did you do?"

"What's that supposed to mean?" Jayson asked.

Morty took another sip of his coffee and told him, "I've known you both since you were kids. You think we all don't know what's going on?"

One of the things that Jayson loved and hated about Sweetbriar is that everyone knew each other...and about each other.

"How does everyone find out about these things so quickly?" Jayson asked.

Morty took a bite of his blueberry muffin and turned to Jayson. "It's Sweetbriar. Everyone knows everything around here. You should have told her."

Jayson rolled his eyes and began to walk to the managing editor's office. "Thanks, Mort."

"I'm just getting used to seeing you around here. I hope she keeps you around," Morty yelled.

He could see her sitting at the desk from the window.

She was talking on the phone while typing furiously on the computer.

He would normally know if she was in a good or a bad mood from the expression on her face, but it had been years. His guess was as good as anyone else's.

She saw him in the window and motioned for him to come in.

"Okay, honey. I have to go. I'll talk to you later. Love you too," she said, hanging up the phone.

"Sorry, it was my fiancé. Have a seat," she told him.

She looked professional in a short-sleeved, gray shirt dress with navy sandals. Her hair was down, the soft waves framed her face. Her scent was something he always remembered and loved. It was a hint of freesia and pink peony.

He sat across from her, nervously placing his hand on his knee.

"I wanted to tell you that Morty sent over the edited copy of the Founders' Day sports feature you did and I loved it. You did an excellent job," she praised him.

Jayson took a deep breath. He was relieved that this was all she wanted to talk to him about.

"So glad you liked it," Jayson said nervously.

"I did. Wanted to go over what you'd want to work on next. Any thoughts?" she asked.

He looked at her strangely. *Was she serious right now?* he wondered. *What was going on?*

"I haven't really thought about it. To be honest, I thought that you were going to let me go," he admitted her.

Kat chuckled. "The thought crossed my mind. But, at work, I'm a pro. And like I said, you have potential. I'd like to see you do these columns on a regular basis. I know we thought of this one occasion. But I'd like you to consider doing this maybe once a week."

Jayson was surprised. He loved writing the article about his family, but he didn't know if he could bring something to the table all the time. Not like that.

"I don't know, Kat," he said hesitantly. "I don't know between playing and practice if I'll be able to. "

Kat looked a little disappointed. "Wow, I wasn't expecting that. I don't say this to a lot of people, but you are talented. You are more than a hockey player. You have chops, like your dad. Actually, you're like an extreme hybrid between Ian and your dad. If you are looking for something to do after your hockey career ends, give sports writing a try," she told him.

He was blown away. "I really didn't think this conversation was going to go this way. I'm floored. I appreciate it. "

Kat smiled. "I don't know how long you are on the injured list, but feel free to keep writing for as long as you want."

"I have a few months yet," he shared as he got up.

"Good! Do me a favor and write a list of the things you'd like to do and I'll meet with Morty and we'll work on them with you." Jayson was still speechless. All of this professionalism was nice, but a bit scary. He was literally ready to be fired or have something thrown at him. Not this calm, cool and collected person who was in front of him.

"Are we going to talk about what happened?" he asked her.

"Yep. But not right now," she told him pointedly.

"Listen, I should have—"

"I have to make some calls," she interrupted him. "We'll talk soon, okay?"

He decided to leave before World War III erupted.

"Okay. I'll be down the hall if you need me."

She put her glasses on and went back to her computer.

He began to walk down the hall. He heard a small sniffle and turned around and noticed she had put her head down. She was sobbing uncontrollably.

It took everything for him to not go to her. But he knew her, she needed to go through what she needed to go through and then they'd talk.

He quietly walked back to his cubicle. He and Morty spent the remainder of the day on plans for the other stories he had in mind.

.

Chapter 27

A couple of weeks later, Michael McKinnon decided to visit *The Post.*

The place that he loved for so long had become a burden for him.

He hated that. He missed crafting a story, talking with people about the things they were going through.

All of the day-to-day meetings with businesses to discuss advertising contracts or discussing subscription numbers made him go blank.

As much as he felt horrible for being responsible for *The Post's* cash flow issues, he was interested to see how Kat was doing. All of these online and mobile apps were great advances, but he knew the townspeople of Sweetbriar.

They would at first be a little curious, but then, like with every new thing that would be the 'in' thing, it would slowly go away.

He walked into the lobby and ran into Lois.

"Michael! How are you feeling?" she asked as she greeted him with a smile and a hug.

He was pleased to see her. "I'm on the mend. Still have a few months before I can come back," he told her. "I thought that I would come and visit my daughter and everyone else."

Lois smiled with pride. "Kat has been doing a fantastic job. Wait until you see the latest figures. Advertising is increasing by the day," she told him.

Michael was a little skeptical. "That's good to hear. But, let me ask you, don't you think all of this progress with being online is temporary?"

Lois giggled. "Oh, not at all. Pretty much every newspaper is online these days. And the companies that we do have as advertisers, Kat and Ross have signed them to long-term agreements."

Michael's eyes raised. "Oh really?"

Lois said, "Kat and Ross can go over the figures with you, if you want."

"I'll go upstairs and talk to her now," he told her as he walked past her and got on the elevator.

When he got upstairs. He noticed that the newsroom was bustling. People were typing away on their computers, consulting with editors, and talking on the phone.

"There is nothing like the hum of the newsroom to get the blood pumping," Ian said to him.

Michael smiled at his star reporter and gave him a hug. "How's it going, Ian?"

"Not bad. Just wrapping up my Founders' Day story."

"Oh nice," Michael said.

"How are you feeling?"

"Feeling better. I lost thirty pounds so far."

Ian smiled. "Look at you! That's great, Mike."

"Yeah, no more double bacon burgers. No cream puffs. Just salads, veggie burgers, and walking a couple times for forty-five minutes a day."

"It's worth it though. You are here with us," Ian told him.

"Thank you for saving my life, by the way. I understand that it was you who called 911 that day."

"My pleasure. Please don't have any more heart attacks. We need you," Ian said.

"I promise. I am done with that. How's Kat doing?"

Ian smiled widely. "She's doing great. We all love her. Have you met her boss, Ross, yet? He's here to help her out with things."

"No, I haven't. I'll make sure I talk with him."

Ian looked at his watch. "Oh, I better go. I have to cover a town meeting. It's good to see you, Mike."

"You too, Ian," Michael told him as he walked up to his office.

Kat was sitting at his desk with Ross talking across from her. The two were laughing as Michael knocked on the door. "Are we getting work done?" he quipped.

Kat smiled and ran over to him. "Daddy! What are you doing here?" she asked.

"Had to see my girl in action. I'm hearing great things," he replied.

"Things are going pretty well. We're looking at a draft of the Founders' Day edition. We sold out our ad space, by the way." She beamed.

Michael said, "So, I heard. Lois and Ian filled me in on that. That's great, honey."

"Thanks, Daddy. Everyone here really came together. You have an amazing team here."

"Sure do," he confirmed.

"Dad, have you met my boss from the *Empire Post,* Ross?" Ross stood up and excitedly went over to him. "Ross, this is my father—"

Ross interrupted, "The Michael McKinnon. You sir are a civil rights icon. It's an honor to meet you."

Michael shook his hand. "Nice to finally meet you. I've heard nothing but great things about you."

"Aww, your daughter is amazing. The way she has swept in and has slowly turned things around. You should be very proud of her," Ross told him.

"I am," Michael shared with him. "I actually wanted to see the progress that you all made."

Kat opened up a drawer and took out a folder. "Here's the preliminary report on ad presales."

Michael's eyes widened. He couldn't believe what he was seeing. "Kat, this is great."

"All of the companies that we have contacted, we've signed to long-term deals. We did a deal with new business owners, like Nicole, who owns Shooter's now, as well as The Hat Trick, thanks to Jayson."

"Jayson?"

"Yes, Jayson actually is who we are calling, The Voice of the Post. He wrote this great story for Founders' Day about his family and their history in town and with the NHL. He's also starting a podcast. His first guest is his dad, Dennis."

Michael smiled. "My man."

"I know, right? Pretty cool."

"Dennis is my best friend and he has refused to be interviewed by everyone, including me and Ian. Jayson's got a gift."

"Well, he's got something. I wouldn't call it a gift," she told her father.

"Oh?" Michael asked

"I think I'll go and grab some soup at that diner you all keep talking about," Ross jumped in. "It was great meeting you, Mr. McKinnon."

"Call me Michael. I feel so old when people call me Mr. McKinnon."

"I hope to see you soon, Michael," Ross said walking out the door.

"What's going on?"

"Jayson lied to me again. Apparently, he never slept with Nicole years ago."

Michael took a deep breath and looked down at his feet.

"Don't even tell me you knew, Daddy?" Kat yelled.

Michael shut the office door.

"I didn't find out until after you left. "

"What the heck? Does the whole town know that I was duped? God, I feel so stupid. I had just begun to trust him again and then there's this."

"Go easy on him. It was a long time ago," Michael told her.

"Go easy on him? He didn't lie to you," she retorted.

"He wanted you to live up to your potential, honey. Look at you. You're a successful writer, you have money, you got a great guy."

"Why didn't anyone let me choose the direction my life was going?"

"Because you wouldn't have been able to help turn this paper around if you had stayed. You wouldn't have a fab life in the city" Michael told her.

Kat looked at the desk for a few seconds. She took out a newspaper and gave it to him. "What's this?" he asked.

It was an edition of the *Empire Post*. On the front page of the Lifestyle section was a photo of Jacques Primeau and his daughter's byline.

"Is this who I think it is?" Michael said with excitement.

"I was going to surprise you for your birthday, but then you had to go and have that heart attack. So, I decided to wait to give it to you when you were up to it," she told him.

Seeing her byline never got old. He grinned from ear to ear. "I can't wait to read this!"

"I can't wait for you to read it too! Interviewing him was magic. He's such a nice guy. Talented."

"All those Friday nights trying to recreate his meals because your mother can't cook for anything."

Kat laughed. "The best times."

"If you had stayed, this interview wouldn't have happened," Michael said.

"I don't know what to do, Daddy."

"Sometimes, as I just realized, it's better to listen than to act," Michael told her.

Kat nodded in agreement.

Chapter 28

Founders' Day was always one of the best days in Sweetbriar. The town had a lot of history. It was known for its diversity.

From sports legends to civil rights icons, the town on this day recognized the past and embraced the future.

What better way to do that than to have *The Post* not only do a commemorative edition, but also host a huge picnic on the bay.

Everyone in town was there. Businesses had booths, the kids played softball and swam in the bay.

It was a beautiful day.

Kat was sitting at *The Post's* booth with her father, Ian, Lois, and Jayson.

Jayson was signing his article, along with some hockey memorabilia for fans.

Kat looked around and smiled. Founders' Day was one of her favorite days in town. She loved the food and everyone coming together. "What nice weather we're having today," Kat noted

She looked cool and comfortable in a blue halter romper and blue sandals. Her hair was down with a blue headband. She wore a pair of designer sunglasses.

"It is nice. Always good to see the town come together," Michael said, as he watched the long line for Jayson as he signed photo after photo.

"You are my favorite player of all time," a little boy told Jayson as he signed a photo and a T-shirt.

Jayson was delighted. "I am! Awesome. What's your name?" he asked the little boy.

"Adam," the little boy told him.

"Well thanks for the compliment," Jayson replied to him.

"I hope you get better soon. We miss you on the ice."

"I'll be back on the ice as soon as I can. In the meantime, you'll see me around town. I own The Hat Trick with my brothers."

"Nice, I'll tell my mom!" the little boy said as he walked away.

"Hey, Adam, if you go to The Hat Trick, make sure you tell one of the staff that you know me, lunch is on me," Jayson told him.

The little boy's eyes lit up. He was grinning from ear to ear. "Thanks, Jayson! See you soon!"

"Aww, that was so sweet," Michael said.

Kat glanced over at Jayson and muttered, "Hope he's not lying to that kid like he did with me."

Michael tapped his daughter on her shoulder and whispered, "Now isn't the time."

Kat shrugged. "Of course not. It's never the right time."

Jayson glared over at her. "Really? Now?" he said to her.

Her phone rang. She looked at it and it was Mitchell. She looked over at her father. "I gotta take this, it's Mitchell."

"Saved by the ring," Jayson said to Michael, who chuckled.

Kat got up and walked away from the booth. "Hello?" she answered.

"Hey, babe! How's it going today?"

"It's going okay. How are you?" she asked.

"I hear a lot of kids and people? Where are you?"

"Oh, it's Founders' Day here in Sweetbriar. Our paper is sponsoring a huge picnic on the bay."

"Oh, nice. So, things are improving since you are sponsoring stuff? Going to be home soon?"

Kat looked perplexed. "Um, not yet. I'll be here for a bit. We have the Harvest Festival and some other things to take care of. Dad's still recuperating," she explained.

"Someone else can do all of that, Kat. You have a home here," he told her.

Kat's eyes narrowed. "Well, I just got a second home here. I can't leave my family."

"Not saying that. Your grandmother can hire other people to take care of things at that newspaper. I miss you," he retorted.

"Well, I miss you too. But my grandmother needs me. I was raised at this newspaper. She and my father taught me everything they know! Just because she can hire someone to run things, doesn't mean that she should when she has someone here to help her," Kat snapped.

"I'm sorry. I shouldn't have said that. Guess work and not seeing you is taking its toll. "

"Well, you can always come here for a visit. Sweetbriar is a nice town," she told him.

"I'll think about it," he told her. "I have to go. I have to meet this guy. Closing on another house in the Hamptons."

"Talk to you soon," she told him and promptly hung up.

Her blood was boiling as Thea came up from behind her eating an ice cream cone. She was about to throw her phone on the ground when Thea said, "Don't do it! You'll need that phone."

Kat looked over at her friend. "Give me one reason why I need it?"

"Your house closing?" Thea grinned.

"Candace knows where to find me," Kat retorted.

"An emergency at the paper?"

"Lois or Ian would track me down?" she quipped.

"Well, what if I need you? Or Jake or Jayson needed you?"

Kat sighed. "You make a good point. Jayson is on his own for a bit."

Thea laughed. "Still not talking to him?"

"Besides an occasional grunt or a snide remark? Not much. I will say that on a professional front, he's got writing chops. His column on his family's origins here until now was fantastic!"

"It was! I didn't know he had that in him. He really did a great job with that," Thea agreed.

"I actually told him that I'd like him to continue doing columns here at *The Post*."

Thea was pleasantly surprised. "Really? What did he say?"

"He said he'd think about it. I get that he's probably going to go back to play and it may be too much with practice and games."

"Well, his contract is up soon. Let him think it over," Thea suggested to her.

"Yeah. In the meantime," Kat said looking at her ring. "Mitchell. He's turned into such a jerk lately. He told me just now that my grandmother should hire someone to run the paper because he misses me and feels like I should come home!"

"Well, what are you going to do after your father comes back? I see his point a little bit. Your job is at the *Empire Post*."

"My job right now is to run things here. I can't let my family down when things are slowly getting better."

Thea took a lick of her ice cream cone. "Of course not."

"I just don't know about Mitchell lately," Kat told her.

"Maybe, he's having a bad day. Don't let him ruin what you've done here today. I mean practically everyone in town is here. They're buying those copies. Jayson's signing them."

"People are also liking the new, updated look for the paper. They are subscribing again." Kat smiled.

"See? This is why you need that phone. Who would you call to tell all that great news to?" Thea asked.

Kat chuckled. "You're a mess."

"Always," Thea said.

Chapter 29

Nicole was running late to the Founders' Day picnic. It was normally not unusual for her to be late, however this time, she had good reason. She was placing the finishing touches on the grand opening of Shooter's after the picnic.

She was proud. She worked hard to prove herself to everyone. She went from being known as the troublemaker who slept with Kat McKinnon's boyfriend, to the new owner of a beloved bar.

She would never forget the kindness that Mr. Shooter gave her.

He gave her a job when no one else would. She had just got out of a disastrous marriage with a drunk and had a newborn to boot. Her grandmother and now adult siblings were too busy this time around with their own lives to have them worry about her latest mess up. So, she let Mr. Shooter show her the ropes of the bar. She waited tables, went to bartending school to learn to mix drinks, business school to learn the business. She paid for everything via tips and help from Mr. Shooter.

She knew Mr. Shooter was sick, but he never let it show. When he passed away, no one was more surprised than her when she found out that he left her the bar.

She got grants and a small business loan and upgraded everything, from the bar to the registers.

Shooter's no longer looked like the local hole-in-the-wall, it looked like an upscale bar you'd find in a major city.

She wore a pair of gray jeans and a light pink T-shirt. Her brown hair was in a ponytail. Her son slept quietly in his stroller as she went through the crowd.

Everyone stopped and greeted her with respect.

"Hi, Nicole," said Lois. "The bar looks great. Looking forward to tonight," she told the young woman.

Nicole smiled. "Thank you. Can't wait for everyone to see it. "

She walked by Kat and Thea, who were talking in front of *The Post's* booth.

"Hi, Nicole!" said Kat, walking over to her.

"Hey, Kat," Nicole replied.

Nicole looked over at Thea with caution. She knew Thea was with Jacob and didn't want any issues. Especially, today.

"Hi, Nicole. Congrats on Shooter's," Thea said with a smile. "It looks great."

Nicole was relieved.

"Thank you, Thea. I hope you both will be at the grand opening tonight. We have a band, line dancing, a bunch of stuff," Nicole told them.

Both ladies nodded. "Definitely!" Kat said.

"Kat told me that it looks amazing in there! I can't wait to see it," Thea chimed in.

Nicole took a deep breath. "I have to admit, I am so nervous. Between getting Griffin to nap and putting the finishing touches on the bar, I want to make sure that everything is perfect."

"It will be. You got this!" Kat reassured her.

"Thanks, Kat. And thanks for all the support *The Post* is giving Shooter's. I really appreciate it."

"My pleasure. Hard work pays off," Kat told her.

"See you both tonight," Nicole said as she walked away.

She ended up being in front of Jayson as he was signing everything in front of him.

He was still stunning. Those hazel eyes, the dark hair, the athletic build. It was as if time stood still.

She hadn't seen him since that day. She was amazed that he still took her breath away after all this time.

She grabbed a copy of the paper and slowly placed it on the table in front of him.

He probably didn't even remember her. It had been years.

"Nicole?" Jayson said as if he had seen a ghost.

She smiled nervously. "Hi, Jay, I was hoping that you could sign this for me?" she said. "I thought it'd be a nice keepsake for my son."

Jayson looked at the little boy and smiled. "What's his name?"

"Griffin. After my late grandfather," she told him.

Jayson chuckled. "He is fast asleep. So cute."

"He's a handful, that's for sure."

Jayson signed the copy and Nicole started to walk away. Jayson got up and went after her.

"Hey, hang on," he told her.

Nicole stopped and turned toward him.

Out of breath, Jayson said, "Listen, I need to apologize to you. I tried to a while ago, but you disappeared after that night."

"I was ashamed of what I did," she admitted to him.

"It wasn't your fault," Jayson assured her.

"I could have told you no," Nicole said. "Kat was always nice to me. I was so jealous of her back then that I couldn't see straight."

"I led you on. That's on me," Jayson told her.

"I would have done it whether you did it or not. Back then, I wanted everything Kat had. She was popular, well off, talented, and she had the guy. The guy who was always nice to me, listened to me, and understood me."

Jayson chuckled. "You and I weren't so different back then. It's probably why I understood you."

"What are you talking about? You were the golden boy. The McQuayde brothers could never do any wrong in this town."

Jayson snickered. "All that glitters ain't gold, Nicole. Again, I'm sorry. You deserve better. I hope you get better. You're a great person. Good luck with the bar tonight," he told her as he walked away.

Nicole felt relieved. For the first time, she felt that she could hold her head up high. Everything was forgiven. She had a brand-new start. She would make sure that she made the most of her new beginning.

Chapter 30

A couple of weeks later in Sweetbriar, the early peaceful morning of the coastal town was replaced by a loud stereo system.

It crackled through the air as if it were a pistol.

People weren't used to that here. At least not that early.

A Black Mercedes convertible roared through Main Street and parked in front of McQuayde's Bakery.

Melissa McQuayde, Jayson, Jacob, and Ian's mother was just starting her day. She was just putting in some bread with her assistant, Jen, when she heard a knock at the door.

Dressed in a blue baker's outfit with her long brown hair wrapped in a bun, she and her other workers attempted to ignore knocking.

"Would you like me to answer that, Melissa?" Jennifer asked.

Melissa rolled her eyes. "No, it's obviously someone who can't read," she told her assistant with a smile.

"Is Shooter's open this early?" Jennifer asked.

Melissa nodded. "I don't think so. Nicole closed it down at two. It's not even 6 a.m. Let's start the cinnamon rolls and see if the breakfast biscuits are ready. People will be coming in at 6:30," she instructed. Her assistant, Jennifer, had her long blonde hair wrapped in a bun. She wore a pink baker's outfit. Jennifer had been with Melissa for years. Melissa relied on her a great deal.

"I'll get those rolls started, Mel, and see if those sausage biscuits are ready," Jennifer told her as she walked into the back.

The knock began again. Only this time, it was louder.

Melissa was walking toward the front of the bakery. She turned the light on. She walked over to the door and saw a very handsome man knocking hard.

"We're closed," she told him.

"What?" the man asked. He had gray eyes and beautiful café au lait skin.

"I said, we're closed. We open at 6:30 a.m.," Melissa yelled through the door.

"But, ma'am, I've been driving for hours. Can't you make an exception?"

Melissa was getting aggravated. "No, we'll be open in a few. If you want, just wait in your car or come back," she told him.

The young man had a designer shirt on, he went into his pocket and took out his wallet and flashed a hundred-dollar bill at her.

"Now listen, I know that you probably haven't seen money like this before, but you can have all of this and the change, if I can get food and some coffee," he insisted.

"No," she replied. "We're closed." And she walked away from the locked door and into the back where Jennifer and the other workers were making and checking the various baked goods for the day.

"Everything okay?" Jennifer asked a frustrated Melissa.

"Yeah, just some jerk who thought that because he had some money, he could buy his way in here to get some food."

Jennifer shook her head. "Unreal."

"The arrogance. I told him that we were closed and that we'd be open at 6:30 and he pulls out a hundred-dollar bill and says, 'I know you haven't seen money like this before but you can keep all of it if you let me in.'"

Jennifer and the workers laughed.

"Does he know who your husband and son are?"

"Obviously not," Melissa said. "It's enough to tick me off."

"Aww, Melissa. Don't let him bother you. He's probably some spoiled rich guy from the city who's used to getting everything he wants."

Melissa wiped her tired eyes and took a deep breath. "You're right. Let's finish up everything before the breakfast crew gets here. Jen, can you send some pies later over to The Hat Trick? Jacob placed their usual order last night."

Jennifer nodded. "Of course," she told her boss. "By the way, how's Claire and Michael?"

Melissa raised her eyebrows. "Oh, I have to bring over some wheat bread for Michael. Michael is doing pretty well. He's lost thirty-five pounds so far."

Jennifer smiled. "That's fantastic. Thank God Kat came in to help out with *The Post*."

Melissa nodded. "Yes, she's doing amazing, I hear. I actually just redid our advertising contract with her for the next year. Jayson's doing some writing there too."

Jennifer looked at her boss with surprise. "Oh really? How's that going?"

Melissa shrugged. "Your guess is as good as mine. I haven't heard of any bloodshed so that's a good thing. Dennis will be home soon to record a podcast with Jay."

"Oh, fun! "

"Yes, so nice that he's doing it for him. Dennis never liked interviews. Not when he was playing hockey and even until now. Says his work tells you everything you need to know about him." Melissa smiled.

"You've been doing everything with him being gone during the week for so long. Mattie, my husband just started driving a truck during the week, how do you both do it?" Jennifer asked

"I don't know. It's something that we always did. I don't know of any other way. Sure, there were times he was home when he was injured or in between contracts. But you get used to it. I relish when he is home. All we do is laugh. Especially at our crazy kids."

Jennifer started to snicker. "They say absence makes the heart grow fonder."

"That it does, Jennifer. That it does," Melissa said as she continued to help the others.

Meanwhile, in the front of the bakery, the young man sat. He looked at himself in the mirror. He was exhausted. He had been driving all night. He couldn't take it anymore. He missed her. He pulled the phone out of his pocket and dialed a number.

"Kat, it's me Mitchell. Just calling to say hi. I know it's early and you're asleep, but I miss you. I guess I'll talk to you later," he said and hung up the phone.

Chapter 31

Later on that morning, Kat was at The Hat Trick. Late the night before, she had texted Jayson to meet her before she went into the office.

She was a ball of nerves. She wanted answers. She just had to know why.

She looked at her phone, it was 7:30 a.m.

The waiter brought over some coffee for the table as she saw Jayson come in. He had a pair of sunglasses on and a pair of black jeans and a gray Henley.

He put the sunglasses in his pocket as he saw her at the booth. She smiled weakly at him.

"Hi," he greeted. Before he sat down, he moved the pot of coffee to the far end of the table.

Kat shot him a peculiar glance as he replied, "I'm moving this for my protection."

She rolled her eyes. "Fine. Thanks for meeting me," she told him.

He sat down across from her. "What's up?" he asked.

"You tell me. Why?" she asked.

"Why what?"

"Why did you do it?" she asked.

"You deserved better," he admitted to her.

"Said who? she asked him. "I loved you. And I thought you loved me too."

"I do—" He corrected, "I did."

Kat was perplexed. "Then help me understand because I'm confused."

Jayson took a long, deep breath. He must have stared at her for several seconds before he found the words.

She started to pick up a cup off the table and he grabbed her hand. She put the cup down.

"I loved you. God, I loved you. Probably too young to love you like I did, but I did. Your talent needed to be on a bigger scale. I remember that story that you wrote while you worked for your grandmother at *The Post* in our junior year and it blew me away. It blew us all away."

"Which one?" she asked.

"The story on the Vietnam vet's medal that you found. "

Kat was surprised he mentioned that. She hadn't thought about that in years. It was the first story she had ever written for anyone before. She looked sad. "Oh, it's been years since I've thought about that medal. I had hoped for a happier ending. You were a big help with that."

"I was hoping the guy who deserved that would have been alive too. But see, that's what I'm talking about. That story grabbed everyone. It wasn't some normal everyday story, it had heart and soul. You wanted to know if that solider was alive or dead."

"But what did that story have to do with you faking sleeping with Nicole?"

"When Syracuse offered you a spot and you didn't want to even think of going because of me, I couldn't let that happen. You were too talented. That story proved that. Your other work since you've left here has shown that."

"So you pushed me away? You're such a self-righteous ass, Jay."

"How?"

"How? How about not letting me make the decision for myself on if I wanted to stay or go."

Jayson countered, "And you would have stayed. And we probably would have gotten married, maybe had a kid? And in between you would have hated me."

She shook her head. "No. I would have gone to school here and probably wrote books or wrote for *The Post*."

"You were too big for *The Post*. You are even now, but at least, you can run it the way you want to."

Kat was silent as Jayson continued, "Could you have met The Duke and Duchess of Sussex or Steven Spielberg if you hadn't gone to school up north? Look at your dad and your grandmother. They went and proved themselves and then came back, if you had stayed, you would have resented me and divorced me."

"Well, we won't know if that would have happened, will we?" she told him.

"It may have been selfish, but I don't regret it. I was devastated when you left."

"Good," she said. Her eyes filled with tears. "We may have been this super couple in school. But you were one of my best friends. I trusted you. I adored you, I would have done anything for you. I lost more than my boyfriend that night."

"And I didn't? I'm sorry. If I could change things, I would have done it differently. And I should have told you when you were first gone. Everyone told me to tell you. But I honestly thought that after all these years, and since you're getting married, you wouldn't care," he told her.

"Who said I was getting married?" Kat asked him.

He held her left hand to his face and played with her ring finger with her engagement ring on it. "Mitchell. Remember him? "

Kat had literally forgot that she had the engagement ring on. When she thought of Mitchell lately, it was nothing but dread and avoidance. Heck, he called her earlier and she didn't even call him back.

Kat looked at the ring. "Would you believe I forgot?"

Jayson snickered. "Yep. I hope this gives you some closure. Even if we aren't friends anymore, I get it. But I miss you and I'm sorry," Jayson said sadly as he got up. He kissed the top of her head as he left for the door.

Tears ran down Kat's face. She looked up and saw Jacob looking sadly from the counter. She got up and left. She had no idea what to do or how to feel. But at least she finally got an answer, even more than what she bargained for.

Chapter 32

"So, how did it go?" Thea asked Kat over the phone. It was her busy season. Proms, bridal work, summer wear. She barely got any sleep this time of year, much less saw anyone.

"Well, he explained it," Kat told her. "Not sure how I feel about it yet. I'm just so angry that he made this decision without me."

"Was there food or drink thrown?" Thea joked.

"No food or drink was sacrificed in our conversation today," Kat replied.

"I get it, Kat. I didn't want to tell you because it wasn't up to me. We all told him that he should be the one to tell you."

"He told me that too. I'm sorry again for jumping all over you."

"I would have too, without knowing everything. It's fine," Thea told her.

"He said he knew I should have gone up north when I did that story on the missing Vietnam vet and his medal that we found. Remember that story?"

"Oh yeah, that was a good story. Sad story, but it was really good," Thea said.

"That story got attention. Dad thought it'd be enough to get some of his friends at Syracuse to give me a shot. I was excited. But I was content to go to Georgia State. I had sent in all of my transcripts and applications. I was just planning on hanging out here and working for *The Post* part time."

"Look at all the of the things you have done since. You're on television. People look to you for every trend."

"I get that, Thea. And I worked hard for that. But, think about it, is learning how to thread your eyebrows or finding out that gray is the next in color really important in the scheme of things? Yes, I got to interview some really cool people. Wasn't it worth it to talk to me, instead of doing what he did, at the very least?"

"You have made a great career out of being an influencer and journalist. I couldn't see you just sitting at home while Jay played hockey, doing the bare minimum. That's not you either, Kat," Thea told her.

"Out of all of that, he reminded me I was engaged and I had a great life in the city. I had pretty much forgotten about my ring."

"Oh? Still grappling with that?"

"Girl, he called before 6 a.m. this morning. I wasn't about to answer that phone. We have to get ready for the Harvest Festival in a couple of months. I have meetings all afternoon about that."

"Good God. Unless, he's dying, why call you that early?" Thea asked.

"My point. I just dread when he calls now. I have to figure this all out. Maybe he isn't the one after all."

"If you are dreading talking to him, then you already have your answer," Thea told her.

"Guess so," Kat agreed. "Thanks for checking up on me."

"Of course," Thea said.

Mitchell still hadn't let Kat know he was in town. He was tired and decided after driving around to check himself in at a hotel.

This town was nothing like he was used to seeing. There were no large skyscrapers or mass transit. The closest mass transit he saw was a bus that looked like a school bus. Everything else around town seemed to be within walking distance. It was quaint and too quiet for him.

Driving up the street, he pulled into the Sweetbriar Inn. The place looked more like a huge plantation than a hotel, but for him, whatever worked. He was tired, he needed a shower, he needed to find Kat.

He got out of the car and went in. The place was clean and it seemed busy. The Inn was run by Claire McKinnon's sister, Maggie, and Kat's younger sister, Natalie, or Nat has everyone called her.

Nat, looked very similar to Kat. She had that trademark long hair and brown eyes. The only difference was that she was a lot quieter, and shorter in stature. Nat sat at the desk with her back turned looking at reservations when he walked up.

"Kat, what are you—"

Nat turned around. She interrupted him and chuckled, "It's not Kat, Mitchell."

Mitchell laughed. "Natalie! I'm so sorry, I need a room. How are you?" he asked.

Nat looked at the computer. "Let me see what I can do."

"I need your best one. I'll pay anything," he told her.

"Hold on, Mitchell. I'll be right with you. Let me check them in first," Natalie replied to him. A young couple came up next to him and he smiled back.

"Reservations for Smith?" the young man said.

Natalie smiled widely. "Well, congratulations Mr. and Mrs. Smith, the Governor's Suite is waiting for you," she told them.

"Thanks so much!" the young woman said.

"You'll love it. It's roomy, has a bar, living area, great views of the bay. "

"Fantastic! I've heard such great things about this place," the young man said.

"Well, we hope you enjoy your stay. Let me go and grab your keys, we're a little short-staffed today. I'll be right back."

Mitchell looked at the couple. That room to him sounded amazing. "Hi there, I guess congratulations are in order." he told the couple grinning from ear to ear.

"Thank you. We just got married earlier," the young man told him.

"That's fantastic. I'm actually here to see my fiancée."

"Oh great!" the young woman said.

"Yes, it's a surprise. She's doesn't know I'm here yet. Quick question, how much did you pay for your room?" he asked.

The young couple looked confused. "Excuse me?" the young man said.

"Your room. Whatever you paid for it; I'll pay double," he told them.

"Um, sir, we got this room a year ago. There was a waiting list," the young woman shared.

"You can't just get this suite," the young man told him. "This is a four-star inn."

"Exactly why I'll pay double," Mitchell informed him. "I'm sure they have other suites here that are equally as nice."

Nat arrived with the couple's keys. She could feel the tension between the two men.

"Here's your keys, Mr. Smith," Natalie said.

"Miss, I'd like to report him. He's harassing us about our suite," the young man complained.

Natalie's eyes raised. She glared angrily at Mitchell, who rolled his eyes and chuckled. "Now, now. I wasn't harassing you. I apologize."

"You tried to buy our suite. It took us a year to book this reservation," the young woman said.

"Mitchell, you need to leave now." Natalie turned to him.

"What? Nat, you got it all wrong."

Nat turned to the couple. "Mr. and Mrs. Smith, as one of the owners of the hotel. I would like to extend my apologies. Anything that you would like on your first night, is on us."

"Why thank you," the young man said.

Natalie replied, "It's the least we can do. We'll have someone bring your bags up to your room."

"Thank you," the young woman said to Natalie, as the couple walked away.

Natalie was angry and turned to Mitchell. "The hell, Mitchell? What is wrong with you?"

"It wasn't like they were saying," he defended to Natalie. "They weren't telling the truth. I was just congratulating them on their marriage and then we got into a little argument. I apologize for any confusion. Do y'all have any rooms?" he asked.

"Actually, we don't," Natalie confirmed "We are completely booked. Summer is our busiest time of year. There is a Super 8 in the next town over in Brighton. I'd try there.

"Well, what about Kat?"

Natalie shrugged. "What about her?"

"If she knew that you refused her fiancé. Well, she'd be pissed."

Natalie rolled her eyes. "She wouldn't. She knows how it works here. We are booked, Mitchell. We can't boot someone just because you're dating my sister!" she said with her voice raised.

"Okay, okay. It's all good," he said as he looked around the inn. Everyone was staring at him. "I'll go to the Super 8. Just tell Kat I was here, okay?"

Natalie nodded as she watched Mitchell storm out.

Chapter 33

Kat spent most of the afternoon in pre-advertising meetings regarding the Harvest Festival. Next to Founders' Day, the Harvest Festival was one of the best advertising days for the paper. The festival was usually held in the town square and all of the businesses in town participated. There were games, food, and dancing. It marked the fall season for Sweetbriar.

"It's been a few weeks since Founders' Day. How are the preliminary figures?" she asked the department heads in the conference room.

"Advertising did well. We got some new business from Shooter's, The Hat Trick, and Stafford's BMW and Starbucks. All of them signed deals for the next year," Lois shared.

Kat was delighted. "That's great! That should put a huge dent in that debt," Kat said.

"Subscriptions are going up thanks to the Friendsbook page. The new website and the mobile app should help us out a lot with those numbers. We increased it by twenty-five percent over the last month," the comptroller said.

Kat was writing all of this down, along with getting the printed reports from everyone. "Nice." She grinned. "I'll ask Ian how his friend is doing on the app. When I saw it last month, the guy was working out the bugs. The website is nearly done. Ross and I have some of the reporters doing exclusive web and mobile content to drive people to the app and the site. We'll also have some of the bigger things like Jayson McQuayde's columns under the paywall," she informed everyone.

"Look at you with the paywall," Ross teased.

Kat snickered. "I'm learning. You're a good teacher."

"You're doing a great job, Kat," Lois said. "Mae has to be proud of you. It's great to see the newsroom buzzing again, and new business coming into *The Post*."

"I hope she is. She loved what we did with Founders' Day. We just have to prove it even more with the Harvest Festival. She'll be looking carefully. The festival is usually, next to Founders' Day, the biggest advertising opportunity for *The Post*. We have to prove that this paper should stay in the family," she told everyone.

"What do you have in mind for the Harvest Festival?" Ross asked.

"First instead of it being in fall, it's being moved up a bit. We'll do another commemorative edition. But we'll focus on new launches, Thea should have a new launch for back to school and homecoming, and Melissa could do a demo on pies. Maybe Jayson wants to talk about what to look for in the upcoming hockey and football season? "

"I like it," Ross said. "Usually it's spring that's the renewal period. For the theme it's Fall Awakening."

"Exactly. We can get Ian to talk to everyone about what they like to do for fall. And I think that I'll chime in and see if I can get a special guest to come in for the festival."

Everyone's face lit up. "Who do you have in mind?" Lois said.

"Jacques Primeau. We are still talking after that interview. He'll actually be in Atlanta the week of the festival; I'll see if he'd want to come down and host a chili cookoff or something."

"I love it!" Lois shrieked.

"I do too! Maybe Jayson can ask some of his hockey friends as well?" Ross asked.

Kat looked down at her pad and wrote some things down. "I can ask him."

"How did your talk go with him earlier?" Lois asked.

Kat looked at her oddly. "How did you know I was talking to him today?"

"It's Sweetbriar, Kat. You think people didn't see you two at The Hat Trick yakking and holding hands."

Kat rolled her eyes. "I forgot how this town has ears."

"So, now that we know. How did it go?" Lois asked her. "I only ask because he works here now. We need things to be professional."

"I agree. It went okay. What's going on with us won't affect *The Post*. In fact, a few weeks ago, I offered him a permanent part-time role. His column did very well and Ross was right. Him being our 'voice or spokesperson' has helped readership. People enjoyed his column."

"Good to hear. It'd be great if he takes it."

"Well, we'll see. Eventually, he'll have to go back to the city and start playing again. He was worried about his schedule and keeping up everything."

"Well, we have a couple of months yet. In the meantime, we can go over all of the ad rates for the Harvest Festival edition." Lois said as they all began to go over the rates and deadlines.

"What in the heck did you say to Kat earlier?" Jacob asked Jayson at The Hat Trick. Jayson was in the back helping out Jacob with some paperwork.

"I told her everything. Why I did what I did, everything," Jayson told him as he was writing stuff down at his desk.

"She looked so confused. She was crying," Jacob informed him. "I never saw her like that before."

"She thinks I was selfish for not letting her decide on going to school."

"Well..." Jacob teased.

"If that were Thea, what would you have done?"

"Um, Thea went to fashion school in Los Angeles for a couple of years and we managed it just fine. Was it easy? No. But, we worked it out."

"I totally forgot she did that," Jayson said.

"That's because you were too busy playing God with Kat's life at the time when Thea left. You were a mess."

"I told her that too. I told her that she didn't do anything. I did love her. I loved her very much. But I just couldn't let her stay, Jake. I couldn't."

"I get it. But did you have to fake sleeping with someone to get her to go?"

"If I knew what I know now? No. But I would have made sure she went to Syracuse."

"Ever think about what would have happened if she did stay?" Jacob asked.

"All the time. You think she hates me now? It would have been fifteen times worse if she had stayed. She would have resented me. I couldn't have lived with myself if I hadn't let her have a shot at her dreams."

"I wonder sometimes if Thea stayed in Los Angeles, would we still be together?" Jacob said.

"And?" Jayson asked.

"No. I wouldn't stand in her way."

"See? I know I upset her. I hope now she and I can get past this and be friends. Giving her some time on that," Jayson said.

"Don't take too long. Time doesn't stand still," Jacob told him.

Chapter 34

A few days later, Kat decided to go to McQuayde's Bakery and grab a blueberry muffin before work. It seemed that with each day, while things at *The Post* were improving, other facets of her personal life were getting more confusing by the day.

She thought about what Jayson had told her a few days ago. He was right. She wouldn't have been able to be as successful as she had been if she would have stayed here. Maybe, since everything was finally out in the open, they could restart their friendship.

Then there was Mitchell. When she finally did return his call, he didn't answer. When he called back, it was so late that she wasn't about to return his call.

She walked into the bakery and the smells of the freshly baked goods were intoxicating.

"Good morning, Kat, what can I get you?" Jennifer, Melissa's assistant, asked. Jennifer was at the counter checking people out at the register.

"Hey, Jen, can I have a blueberry muffin for myself and a dozen chocolate muffins for the office?" Kat asked.

"Coming right up!" Jen said as she went into the back to get them, she walked past Melissa who came up front.

"Hey, Kat! How are you?" Melissa asked.

"Hey, Mrs. McQuayde. I'm doing great, thanks."

"Are you being helped dear?" Melissa asked.

Kat nodded. "Yes, Jen is grabbing some muffins for me."

"Perfect! So, things are okay? How's your dad? I haven't talked to your mom in a couple of days."

"Dad is doing great. He can't wait to see Mr. McQuayde soon."

Melissa chuckled. "Aww, Den adores your dad. Glad he's doing well."

"Yes, he is. He's down thirty-eight pounds and now has been telling us to get some exercise in every day."

Melissa started to laugh. "Well, would you look at that! Not too long ago we couldn't get him away from those cream puffs!"

"See, there are miracles."

"We have a lot of low sugar options for your dad, all your mom has to do is say the word. Your father won't ever know the difference."

"I'll let her know. Thanks."

"Everything okay at the paper? How's my son working out?"

Kat took a deep breath and looked at her.

"Ruh oh. I know that look. What did he do now?" Melissa asked.

"I'm sure you know the real reason he ended things with me?" Kat asked.

Melissa walked around the counter and toward Kat. She took Kat over to a table in the far end of the room and sat her down.

"I was wondering when you would find out," Melissa said in a low voice.

"I found out from Nicole. I was talking with her about doing some advertising for Shooter's and she told me."

Melissa looked grim. "I hated he did that to both of you girls. Nicole always had a crush on him. I tried to tell him that, but he only cared about you and what you thought about things. I know he did love you. He just didn't think it all out."

"Still trying to make it make sense. Not as angry as I was. He and I did talk. I get that he didn't want me to regret not going to school. I just feel—"

Melissa interrupted, "Like he took something from you by not giving you a choice."

Kat nodded. "Yeah. Regardless of how things ended, we were friends."

"I think you can be. Friendships like all things take time. I remember you, Thea, Jayson, and Jake. The four of you did everything together. Those are a lot of memories to cherish," Melissa reminded her.

"Yes, the Four Musketeers. That's what we were called back then."

"Well, if you want to make more memories like that, try to move past it. You may find that you like Jayson even more now as a friend than you did all those years ago."

Jennifer came over with a huge bag. "Here's your muffins. Fresh out of the oven," she told Kat.

"How much do I owe you?" she asked Melissa and Jennifer.

Melissa shook her head. "On the house."

"Thanks, Mrs. McQuayde," Kat said picking up the bag.

"Kat, call me Melissa. We're all adults. You are making me feel old calling me Mrs."

Kat snickered. "Okay, Melissa. I better get going. Thanks for the chat."

"Anytime. Such a pleasant face. Not like the idiot who tried to come in a few days ago."

Kat looked confused. "What happened a few days ago?"

"This moron insisted that I open the bakery for him because he was hungry. When I told him we were closed, he flashed a hundred-dollar bill and said 'I'm sure that you haven't seen this much money before and you can have all of it, if I can just grab some food.'"

Kat raised her eyebrows. "What in the world?"

"I told him no. I haven't seen him since."

Kat shook her head. "Good. We don't need people like him around here. He's probably some rich kid from Atlanta."

"That's what I think too. Oh well, have a great day and tell your mother I'll call her later. We need a girls' night out," Melissa said.

"Will do," Kat replied as she walked out the door. She had a new perspective, thanks to Melissa, on how to try to move forward with Jayson on a new friendship. She would be up to it, but would he?

Chapter 35

"I bring muffins for all!" Kat said as she walked into the newsroom with the bag from McQuayde's Bakery.

Everyone in the newsroom came out of nowhere and watched as she put the muffins on an empty table.

She walked slowly from the table and suddenly they grabbed the muffins as if they had never seen food before in their lives.

Kat chuckled. She had grabbed her blueberry muffin and headed toward her dad's office.

"Hey, Kat, do you have a minute?" a male voice said.

She turned around and saw that it was Jayson following her into the office.

"Not grabbing a muffin?" she asked.

"Nah, I grew up baking those, remember? I know those fattening secrets. I got the clearance to start exercising again, so none of those for a bit."

"Nice! Good for you. Glad to see the knee is better," she told him as she sat down at the desk. He sat across from her.

'Yeah, I'm really happy about it. Which is what I came in here to talk to you about."

Suddenly, her smile turned to sadness. "I have a feeling I'm not going to like this," she told him.

"Well, I still have a couple of months before I go back. But I don't know if I'll be able to do a column and train and play and everything else. I'll be just getting back on my feet again."

Kat looked disappointed. "I understand. Everyone loves having you here. They'll miss you."

"Will you miss me?" he asked.

"Well, I don't know. You kinda put me through it," Kat quipped. "I will. But chances are, I'll be back in New York in a couple of months anyway."

"See, I'm not the only one taking off," he told her.

"This time, I'm not going to be a stranger. In fact, I have to meet Candace this afternoon. I bought the Mulderry Farmhouse and I close on it today."

Jayson's eyes lit up. "No way! We loved that house as kids."

Kat laughed. "Yes, we did. So many good times at that house. It's actually in really good condition. Just have to repaint and fix some fencing and trim up the gardens."

"Well, if you need any help? I'd be more than happy to," he volunteered.

"I may take you up on it. I can use all the help I can get. Maybe, we should get the band together and have a painting party."

Jayson smiled. "Nice, I'll let Jake know, I'm sure Thea would love to get out of prom and bridal land for a day."

Kat laughed. "Poor girl is going through it. I haven't seen her in days. The shop is packed every time I go past it."

"Well, good for her though. She's living her dream," Jayson said.

"She is. She's always wanted to design clothes and own a store. She's really created something great here," Kat told him.

"Yeah. And you? You have a wedding to plan, right?"

Kat rolled her eyes. "Don't remind me. I haven't even begun to think about a wedding. Not with things being the way they are with Dad and *The Post.*"

"Isn't your dad getting better though?"

Kat nodded. "Yeah. He's doing well. I was telling your mom earlier, now Dad is more of an exerciser than all of us. He's the first person to workout. He has completely changed his eating habits."

"Go, Michael. That's fantastic!" Jayson told her.

"Yes, it is. It'll be sad to give this all back to him. It's been fun learning the ins and outs of running things."

"Well, you're doing great. Maybe it's something for you to think about doing later on."

Kat shrugged. "Never really thought about it until just now. I love writing and I love storytelling. But seeing all of the departments of the newspaper come together and form a daily edition that people put their blood, sweat, and tears in gives me a sense of pride. It's like we're all putting together a giant jigsaw puzzle each and every day."

"This is why I did what I did years ago. That look, that drive. You couldn't have accomplished half of this if you had stayed."

"You are right," she told him.

Jayson looked at her with surprise. "Oh, really? "

Kat nodded and smiled. "Don't flatter yourself, but yeah. You were right."

Kat's phone went off. She picked it up and groaned, "It's Mitchell."

Jayson began to get up. "Oh stay," she insisted. "I'm not answering it. All he wants me to do is go back to the city while he tells me about all of his contracts."

"Oh?"

"And then we argue."

"About what?" Jayson asked.

"About me staying here and why doesn't my grandmother hire someone to run things. Besides that, there is just something about him that is bugging me lately. I thought that being away would be good, but it's making me see my relationship with him differently."

"Engagements are supposed to be a happy time," he reminded her.

"Are they? This is my first one," Kat joked.

"I wouldn't know either. But most of the people I know, they're happy to speak with their fiancé," he teased her.

"It's this sense of dread. I literally ask myself. What is he going to talk about today? Another house sale? Another celebrity, himself? "

"Sounds like a guy I want to hang out with," Jayson said sarcastically.

"You'd love him. Not," Kat quipped. "It's the complete opposite of you. When Mitchell and I first met, he was cool. He was just starting out. He was hungry, humble, very sweet. But then, success happened and it changed him. "

"Happens sometimes. What are you going to do?" Jayson asked.

Kat looked at her ring. She took it off and put it down on the desk. "Nothing for now. If anything happens, it'll be when I get back to New York," she told him.

Jayson got up. "Well, you have me for a couple of months at least. I got an idea for a story. I'll send it over to you and Mort in a few."

Kat nodded. "Sounds good."

Jayson began to leave.

"Jayson?" she asked.

He turned toward her. "Yeah?"

"Thanks for listening."

Jayson smiled. "That's what friends do," he told her as he walked back to the sports department.

Chapter 36

Mitchell watched TV in his room at the Super 8 in the nearby town of Brighton, Georgia. The room was nice, but it wasn't the type of room he was used to staying in. He had worked hard to achieve the lifestyle he was accustomed to these days, which was four-star. He had nothing against the Super 8, but he felt as if he didn't deserve to be here.

He looked at the time. These days, he was playing phone tag with Kat. She either was too busy to talk to him or it was too late. He thought that as his fiancée she would be happy to talk to him.

He knew that she shouldn't have gone back home. For Mitchell, every single time she mentioned Sweetbriar, it was about Jayson. The town, from the looks of it, seemed nice but it wasn't like being in the city. It was too small and too primitive in his opinion. To him, everyone had a price. He had learned that when he was raised in the projects. He worked hard to leave that life by hustling. From selling newspapers to homes. The more he sold, the more money he saw. The more money you had, the more you could create the world you wanted. Mitchell was getting everything he wanted. He was a multi-millionaire, he had a great career, and the prize? A beautiful and talented woman by his side.

He picked up the phone. It was 11:30 a.m., he decided to try her. *She should be at her desk,* he thought. *Not running around, no meetings, her dad was home. What else could she be doing?*

He decided to dial her number.

"Hello?" an unfamiliar female voice answered.

"Who's this?" Mitchell asked.

"This is Lois. Can I ask who's calling?"

"Why are you on my girl's phone?" he demanded.

"Who is your girl?" Lois asked in a cool Southern drawl.

"Katherine McKinnon, is she available?" he asked.

"Oh, Kat. No, she's not. She's with the staff getting ready for the Harvest Festival," Lois explained.

"Why are you answering her phone?" he asked.

"Well, she accidently left it here on her desk. I was about to leave myself. I'm the office manager at the paper. Can I take a message?"

Mitchell was disgusted. He was tired of her not answering his calls. "No, she'll see me soon enough. I'm done with this mess," he said as he slammed the phone down on the bed.

This was ridiculous. Now, she was at some generic festival. Sweetbriar was in the next town over. . Maybe by the time he showered and got dressed, she'd still be there by the time he got there.

In Sweetbriar, the town was buzzing with excitement over the Harvest Festival. The annual festival would normally mark the end of summer and into fall. But this year, it was being held to mark a fresh beginning for *The Post*.

Kat, Ross, Ian, and Jayson were helping out with decorations around the town.

"Why are we having a Harvest Festival during summer?" Ross asked.

"To mark a fresh new start for *The Post*. New design, new internet presence, new app, new column," Kat answered.

"And why not. It's an excuse to have a celebration," Ian said while putting up a half flower, half corn husk creation on a lamppost.

"God knows this town likes to have fun," Jayson told everyone.

"Are you excited about interviewing your dad live for your first podcast?" asked Kat.

Jayson nodded. "Actually, I am. A little nervous doing it in front of everyone, but it'll be fun."

Kat reassured him, "It'll be fun. You're with friends. I'm looking forward to it. I know Daddy is too."

"Oh, Kat. Any word on Primeau?" Ross asked.

Kat's eyes glittered with delight.

"Yes, Lois is on her way to the airport to get him as we speak."

"Primeau? " Jayson asked.

"Jacques Primeau. The famous chef?" Kat told him while putting another decoration up on a pole.

Jayson looked at her confused. "Never heard of him."

Ian, Kat, and Ross looked at him with surprise. "Are you serious? Jacques Primeau is one of the best chefs in the world," Ian informed him. "Ever been to The Primrose?"

Jayson nodded. "Yea, it's a great restaurant in New York. Why?"

"That's his restaurant," Kat told him.

Jayson looked surprised. "Oh really? That's his place? Place has great steaks."

Kat shook her head. "Anyway, Jacques is going to be doing a live cooking demonstration."

"Nice! What's he making?" Ian asked

"Not sure. Whatever it is, it'll be great," Kat said. She turned to Jayson, who was standing across from her. "Hey, you should talk to him about The Hat Trick. Maybe he can give you and Jake some advice. Not that you need it."

Jayson shrugged. "Actually, that's not a bad idea. Jake has been thinking about adding a second diner in Brighton. He found a great spot when he was out of town a few weeks ago."

Kat smiled. "That's fantastic. You guys can be a chain!" she squealed.

"Can you imagine?" Jayson said. "It'd be pretty cool. It's great seeing how well the diner is doing."

"Well, ask Jacques for advice. What's the worst he can say ? No?" Kat insisted.

"True," Jayson said. He walked up to her and took her hand. "Hey, you have a sec?"

"Sure," she told him and walked with him across the street. "What's up?" she asked.

"Feeling better about things today?" he asked with some hesitation.

"I'm okay. Why?" she asked.

Jayson appeared nervous. "Listen, if I'm overstepping, please let me know. I know that you were upset with your fiancé the other day and I'm just making sure that you're okay."

Kat looked awkwardly at him and told him, "Yes, I'm okay. I think that when I get back to New York in a couple of weeks that I'll call things off."

Jayson was surprised, but bemused. "Oh that's too bad," he told her.

Kat snickered and rolled her eyes. "Really, Jay?"

Jayson looked at her and grinned. "What?"

"You really feel bad?" she asked.

Jayson's eyes locked onto hers. She looked beautiful in the morning sun. Her hair was in a long braid, she wore a pair of gray jeans and a white shirt.

"Actually, no. Not one bit."

Chapter 37

K at was taken aback by Jayson's answer. It had been years since there was anything between them and yet, he seemed happy that she decided to break things off with Mitchell.

"What did you mean by that?" she asked him.

"Like I said. I'm glad you're breaking things off with him. The guy seems to be stressing you out," Jayson told her as the two began to walk down the street.

Kat looked at him with some suspicion. She didn't know if she should believe him or if there were some underlying motives.

"True. He is stressing me out. But you have this bemused look on your face."

Jayson grinned devilishly from ear to ear. "I do?"

Kat chuckled. "You do."

"Well, I mean it's too bad. Couples should be happy. You deserve to be happy. As a friend, I want you to be happy."

"Are we friends?" she asked.

He couldn't stop looking at her. "Of course. I'm hoping we are after everything. I have nothing to hide anymore. I'm all in with this? Are you?"

There were those two words again. "All in." They either gave her great joy or immense stress.

Considering everything that happened and as much as she wanted things to be like they were, she erred on the side of caution.

"Yeah, sure." She nodded.

"I know you have every right not to trust me. But I just want you to know that I'm on your side with this. We are friends before anything else. "

"Thank you," she told him. "We are friends. I appreciate it. I just need more time. There are some things I can't let you off the hook for immediately, ya know?"

Jayson took a deep breath. "Okay, as long as there's no food or drinks spilled on me, I'm good," he quipped.

Kat teased, "Never say never."

The two walked back across the street to help out Ross and Ian finish up the decorations.

As they did that, a candy apple red pickup rolled up on the side of them. The four of them stared at the truck and watched as the tinted window on the driver's side slowly went down.

The man in the driver's seat gave them a wide smile. He was rugged looking with short silver hair and hazel eyes. The grin was the trademark McQuayde grin.

"So, you all decided to have a celebration for my return. How nice!" he told the group with a hint of Southern twang.

Jayson and Ian laughed. "You wish it was about you," Jayson quipped.

"Welcome home, old man," Ian said.

Dennis McQuayde got out of the truck. The NHL legend, now analyst, had a strong resemblance to his sons. It was something that always took Kat by surprise.

Jayson and Ian walked over to him and hugged him.

"How you guys doing?" Den asked his sons.

Both of them nodded. "We're good," Ian said.

Den pointed at Jayson's knee. "How's it holding up?"

"It's doing a lot better. Getting better every day."

"Rest and ice it every night. The guys miss you, by the way. They can't wait to see you."

"It's looking like September or October," Jayson said.

"Just in the nick of time for the start of the season," Den said with a wink. He looked over at Kat. His eyes gleamed with joy.

"Come here you. I heard there was a rumor you were home," he told her.

She walked over to him and hugged him. "Oh, it's so good to see you. It's been awhile. Dad know you're home?"

"I called him this morning and told him I was rolling in. I can't wait to see him."

"He really misses you." Kat told him.

"We talk like five times a day. I think he's going crazy with boredom," Den informed her.

Kat laughed. "Well, thank God you're here. You can help him get into some trouble."

"Tell your mom to get the bail money ready," he joked.

Dennis looked around the town. "Are we really doing the Harvest Festival now?" he asked.

"Well, yeah. It's more like a relaunch celebration of *The Post*. The paper had some cash flow issues, my friend Ross and I put some things into place to help out with that, and it's working. We updated the look of the paper, it's officially online, and there's a mobile app. And Jayson was nice enough to lend his celebrity in our quest for new subscribers by launching this podcast and a special column."

Dennis looked over at his son proudly. He tapped him on the shoulder. "Well, look at you. Getting ready for the next step of your life," he told him.

Jayson shrugged. "I don't know yet. Maybe?"

"I keep telling him, he's got the chops. He has a home here if he wants one," Kat insisted.

"I have one more season to go, Kat. Then, I'll make up my mind. But for now, you have me," Jayson told her.

"I'm happy about that." She grinned.

"Another McQuayde in the news world is what we need," Ian said. "Got my vote."

"Mine too," Ross agreed with his British accent. He walked up to Dennis with his hand outstretched.

"Hello, I'm Ross Nagles. We haven't been introduced. I'm Kat's boss at the *Empire Post*. I'm helping her out here for a bit until her dad gets on his feet."

Dennis gave him a warm smile as he shook his hand. "Nice to meet you, Ross. Thanks for helping out my best friend and his daughter."

"Anytime. Michael McKinnon and his work were a huge influence on me. I was happy to help him out. His daughter is equally, if not more, talented."

Dennis chuckled. "You're not going to get me to disagree. Kat has always been a talented one. She gets it from her father and grandmother," Dennis said looking at Kat with pride.

"Aww, thank you, Mr. McQuayde."

"Call me Dennis. I feel a hundred when adults do that," Dennis insisted.

"Well..." Ian teased.

"That's enough, Ian," Dennis retorted.

Kat laughed. "Okay, Dennis."

"Hungry, Dad? Want to go to the diner before everything gets started?" Jayson asked.

"I am actually. I already dropped in on your mother. She was busy getting all the pies together for tonight."

"Let's go then."

Chapter 38

Jayson and Ian took their father, Dennis, to The Hat Trick. As usual, the place was busy, not just because of the customers, but also prepping for the festival.

As Dennis and Ian sat down, Jacob went running over to his father.

"Look what the cat dragged in," he greeted his father.

"Look at my son, the businessman," Dennis said as he looked around.

Jayson cleared his throat. "Ahem, um, there were three of us who started this small business."

"Tell 'em, Jay," Ian urged his brother.

"Now, sons, I know the three of you did this together. But Jacob is here the most. It was his baby. Ian, you've got a great career as a reporter. Jayson, you followed in my footsteps as an NHL star but, Jake, you started in the NHL and decided to turn your love of food into something awesome. Proud of you boys." Dennis smiled with pride at all three of his sons.

"What can I get you, Pop?" Jake said.

"Whatever you want, Jake," Dennis replied to his son.

"Okay, one BLT and fries coming up." Jacob told him as he left into the kitchen.

"My man," Dennis said.

The elder McQuayde continued to look around. He couldn't believe how busy the diner was. Jayson sat down across from Dennis and Ian.

"So, what were you talking to Kat about earlier?" Ian asked Jayson.

"Oh, nothing," Jayson answered casually.

"When did you and her start talking again?" his dad questioned.

"Long story," Jayson told him.

"I have a few. Does she finally know about what actually happened that day?" Dennis asked.

Jayson nodded. "Yeah, that was interesting. She found out from Nicole. Nicole now owns Shooter's."

Dennis chuckled. "Oh man. I can imagine how that went."

"Well, I wasn't going to tell you that I told you so. But I'm going to tell you that I told you so," Ian chimed in.

"How bad did it get?" Dennis asked Jayson.

"Well, she threw chicken à ka king on me and then Thea poured soup on me."

Dennis began to laugh. "That could have gone a lot worse and I'm on Team Kat and Thea."

"Thanks for the support, Pop," Jayson told his father.

"Seriously, I'm glad that's all over. For all of us. Your mom and I are close to Michael, Claire, and Mae. Jake and Ian are tight with Kat and her sisters. That whole thing was tense. Not just for you, but for all of us," Den informed Jayson. "That was a mess."

"It was. I take full responsibility. Kat and I are okay. We talked. We decided to take things slow."

"Do you still have feelings for her?" Dennis asked.

Jayson looked awkwardly at his father. "I don't know. I'll always care about her. That was so long ago."

"I heard her arguing with her boyfriend the other day on the phone," Ian said.

"Boyfriend?" Dennis asked.

"Yeah, she's seeing some millionaire real estate guy in New York." Jayson explained to Dennis.

"They're a dime a dozen there," Dennis told him.

"It's Mitchell Simmons," Jayson replied.

Dennis raised his eyebrows. "Oh, that guy is talented. But he's a bit of a jerk I heard."

"I never talked to him. A couple of the guys on the team had him as a real estate agent."

"He apparently tried to buy his way into getting season tickets to the Islanders from a couple of network guys. Needless to say, it didn't go well," Dennis said.

"Sounds like Kat got herself a winner," Ian observed.

"Well, not for much longer," Jayson added.

"Oh?" Ian said.

"Yeah, she told me that she's breaking up with him when she goes back to New York."

"Well, there's your opening, Jay," Dennis told him as Jacob came over with three plates of food.

"What opening?" Jacob asked.

"Kat's breaking up with her boyfriend," Dennis told him.

Jacob smiled widely. "Really?"

Jayson chuckled. "Really."

"The Four Musketeers are going to be back in business!" Jacob told him.

"What? Jake, she and I are friends."

"I've seen the way you look at her. You haven't gotten her out of your system," Jacob pointed out as he sat down next to his fraternal twin.

"Come on, I have. It was years ago," Jayson insisted.

"I don't know. The way you were looking at her while you both were talking earlier had me wondering," said Ian.

"Listen, she's a great girl. She's smart, successful, beautiful. I have fun with her. We always had fun. That's all it is."

"In other words, you have unfinished business to take care of," Dennis insisted.

Jayson was bewildered. "Um, no. There isn't."

"If there isn't, then why are you bending over backward trying to explain this phase of your relationship?" Jacob asked

"Because maybe I'm just friends with her, Jake."

Jacob glanced at him with skepticism. "Nah, I saw you when we were all on that boat together a few weeks ago. You had the same look in your eyes that you had when you were seeing her the first time."

Dennis took a bite of his sandwich and added, "In other words, it's unfinished business."

Ian began to laugh as Jayson put his head down in frustration.

"You guys are a mess," Jayson told them. "I give up."

"As long as you don't give up on her, we've got you," Jacob assured him, patting him on the back.

Chapter 39

Mitchell arrived in town. He looked around and saw that the town was all decorated in various pastel flowers and cornhusks. Despite the coastal town's beauty, he rolled his eyes as he pulled into McQuayde's Bakery.

He figured that since it was early afternoon, this time, he wouldn't be turned away.

He walked in and saw Melissa at the register ringing people up.

She looked at him and pursed her lips. He realized she remembered him from before.

"Hi, can I help you?" she asked.

"Yes, can I have a mini quiche and a caramel iced coffee, please?"

She looked at the counter and saw that the quiches were empty.

"I'm sorry, we're out of the quiches for now. Would you like something else?" she asked.

He rolled his eyes. "No, can't y'all make some?" he asked.

Melissa pulled back. "Well, normally yes we can—"

Mitchell interrupted her, "Your service here is unprofessional. Every time I have come in here, there's some sort of an issue."

Melissa's eyes turned red. "Excuse me?"

"Excuse you? No, you have been awful to me each and every time I have come in here. I want to speak to your manager!" he shouted.

Melissa chuckled out of frustration. "What for?"

"For not giving me what I asked for," he retorted.

"Sir, we don't have any mini quiches at the moment because we are closing early. There is a town festival that we are helping to cater. If you would like mini quiches, there will be plenty there. If you will excuse me, the owner of this place, which is me, has to actually work.

Jen, would you please get this gentleman his iced coffee? And, sir, never come in here again!" she said angrily as she walked into the back.

Thea and Kat were getting ready at Thea's since her place was closer to the town square.

Both ladies were freshly showered. Kat was drying her hair and dressed in a terry cloth robe when Thea came into the bathroom.

"Fresh as a daisy," Thea said to her best friend.

Kat, who was nearly finished with the hair dryer, smiled at Thea in the mirror. "Thanks for letting me dress here. The new house isn't ready yet. "

"Of course. So glad you have that gorgeous farmhouse," Thea told her.

Kat's eyes lit up. "Me too. Nicole was nice enough to give me the guy's name who helped her remodel Shooter's, they'll start on everything tomorrow. New paint, new stones in the back. The landscapers were there this morning, trimming up the overgrowth."

Thea squealed with delight. "It'll be so nice to have you around. Even if it's for a little bit here and there."

Kat began to brush her hair. She gave Thea the hair dryer. "Well, I've been thinking about that..."

"Oh?" Thea said.

"I missed home, Thea. Seeing you and everyone. It's familiar and grounding. Before Dad had his heart attack, my brain was spinning constantly. It was as if I was a hamster and couldn't get off the wheel."

Thea laughed as Kat continued, "What happened put things into perspective. I don't know if I want to go back full time to the city."

"Oh?" Thea questioned her. "Not that I wouldn't mind you being here all the time. But what about your job? And Mitchell?"

Kat took a deep breath. "When I get back, I'm calling things off with him. You were right. Being engaged is supposed to be a happy time, if I'm avoiding him now, how am I going to react if I marry him?"

Thea wrapped her arm around her Kat. "That's my girl. Whatever you decide and with whomever, I'm here for you."

Kat closed her eyes. "Thank you, sweets."

"Better get ready. You know, I like a good party," Thea reminded her.

By the time, the ladies got there, it was early evening. The sky was colored in light blue, pink, and purple hues. The hues matched the pastel peonies and cornhusks that were scattered throughout the town landscape.

Kat wore her hair down. She and Thea were dressed in white linen sheath dresses designed by Thea. Kat's was a halter dress and Thea's had spaghetti straps.

The ladies walked around to admire everyone's booths. Shooter's had a stage where live music played in the center of the square. People were dancing, eating, and having a great time.

Kat said hello to Nicole and Candace and then she saw him.

She was speechless. It was as if time stood still.

He was breathtaking. He was dressed in a pair of khakis and a black shirt. His gray eyes locked onto hers with warmth. She didn't realize how wide she was smiling.

The way he walked over to her; it was as if he was floating on air. Suddenly, there was no one else around but the two of them.

"Hello," Jayson greeted her softly.

"Hi there," she replied. Her eyes never left his.

He observed her dress and smiled. "You look beautiful."

"Thank you. This is one of Thea's designs."

Thea touched Kat's arm and said, "I'm going to try to find my boyfriend."

"He's at The Hat Trick's booth with Dad," Jayson told her as Thea went off.

Kat looked around the town square nervously. Her face felt flushed. "It's a beautiful night."

Jayson nodded. "Yeah, everything turned out great. You should be proud of yourself."

Kat laughed nervously. "Well, it's not just me."

Jayson nodded and winked. "Yeah, it is."

He held his hand out. "Dance with me?"

Her hand shook as she reached for his. She didn't understand what was happening. Why did she feel like she was eighteen again? *Why does he look so good!* she thought.

His fingers weaved into hers. His eyes never wavered from hers.

The two walked toward the front of the stage, he pulled her close to him. "How did the interview go with your dad?" she asked.

"He was hysterical, as always. Everyone seemed to get a kick out of it. I'm surprised you didn't come," he told her. His breath was warm against her face.

"Nah, you had this. You didn't need me," she told him.

"I may not have, but I love when you're around," he admitted.

"Well, you have me here for a couple of more weeks."

"Kat, I don't want you to go," he confessed.

Her eyes locked into his.

"Why don't you want me to go?" she asked.

He looked sad. "I don't want to make the same mistake as before."

"Huh?" she said.

"I was so scared back then. I was scared that if you stayed, you'd leave me or if I left, you'd leave. You are so amazing, Kat. I look at you and I'm in awe. You are an amazing writer, a great friend, and such a great girlfriend," he said with tears in his eyes.

"Jay, it was so long ago. What are you trying to say?" she asked. Her eyes were pleading with his.

"Kat, I—" Suddenly out of nowhere, Mitchell barged in the middle of them and punched Jayson in the face.

Chapter 40

"Mitchell! What are you doing?!" Kat yelled as she went over to Jayson. "Are you okay?" she asked Jayson with concern.

Mitchell was livid. "What am I doing? What are you doing, Kat? Who is he?"

Jayson pushed Mitchell into the crowd. Mitchell hurled at Jayson and threw him down on the ground.

Kat tried to stop it by getting in the middle. "Stop it! Stop it!" she yelled.

Mitchell was so enraged that he mistakenly pushed Kat down on the ground.

"Ouch!" she cried out.

Suddenly, Dennis and Jacob jumped into the middle of the fight to break them up.

"Jayson. Stop!" Jacob said. Mitchell lunged at Jacob.

"Let me at him!" Mitchell shouted.

"What is your problem?" Jayson said. "Kat, are you okay?"

Thea, Kat's mother, Claire, and Candace were consoling Kat as she nodded.

Mitchell turned to Kat, who was crying hysterically and said, "See what you made me do? I came all the way down here and this is what you've been doing behind my back?"

Kat walked up to him and slapped him in the face.

"You asshole! I've done nothing wrong. Jayson is a friend."

Mitchell snickered. "Oh, so this is the great Jayson McQuayde?" he shouted. "I thought you hated him?"

"I was wrong," Kat said as she cried.

"So, now you're going to be with him?" Mitchell said.

"No." Kat nodded. "It's not like that!" she said.

Jayson looked at her with tears in his eyes.

"Then what? You've been avoiding me. You won't take my calls half the time, and when you do, you are always busy."

"In case you don't believe this, I am working. I came here to help out my family. They have a newspaper; I am running things. Sorry, I can't be there to hear you gloat about another contract or how you've hustled another person to get what you want!"

Melissa came over and looked at him. "Oh, it's you!" She pointed.

Mitchell rolled his eyes at her. "Go away, lady!" he told her.

"Don't talk to my mother like that you—" Jayson interrupted as he tried to push his brother to get to Mitchell.

"Mom, what's going on?" Jacob asked.

"This guy came to the bakery a couple of weeks ago and demanded to come in while we were closed. He tried to give me a hundred-dollar bill and said to me that since it's the most money that I've ever seen, I could keep the change if I let him in."

Jacob looked at Mitchell with disgust. "Aren't you a winner?" he told him.

Melissa continued, "And then earlier today, he comes in and has a fit because we couldn't make a mini quiche for him."

Kat's eyes narrowed with anger.

"And he came to the Inn a couple of weeks ago and tried to buy a suite off of a newlywed couple," Natalie shared with her younger sister.

"Are you serious? How long have you been in town?" Kat asked.

"Not the point. I came here to take you home. You belong in the city. You have friends in the music and entertainment industry. You have everything you need there."

"I didn't have home," she said. She took the engagement ring off of her hand and gave it to him. "I believe this is yours."

"You come back with me and we can still own the city, you stay and I'll ruin you by telling everyone that you're a whore," he told her.

Suddenly, someone from behind poured a tub of tomato sauce on Mitchell.

Everyone in the square was silent for several seconds.

"You will say nothing about Katherine," a male voice said with a distinct French accent. He walked up from behind Mitchell who was covered in sauce.

"Says who?" Mitchell said.

The man was tall, handsome, and wore a chef's outfit. He had blue eyes and black hair. "My name is Jacques Primeau. You sold my mother a house that was full of termites. You paid off the house inspector so that it passed inspection during the closing process. The house's structure was nearly gone. The home was uninhabitable."

Kat's eyes widened. She couldn't believe what she was hearing as Jacques continued.

"I don't know what you're talking about, man. You're about to get sued. Look at me!" Mitchell shouted.

"Oh, I'm looking at you. If you say anything about Kat and what happened here today. I'll make sure you lose your license."

"You're lying. You won't do anything." Mitchell snickered.

"You want to make a bet? I know a lot of people, Mr. Simmons, just like you. I can end you with one call. Shall I call the board head now?" Jacques asked as he took out his phone.

Mitchell laughed. "Nah, that's okay. I'm good. I'll leave her alone. She's not worth it anyway. She's just some hick country girl who loves to play rich girl when it's convenient. Do you know how many girls want me? I'll find another, prettier and richer." A man tapped on Mitchell's shoulder. Mitchell turned and got a punch in the face. It was Kat's father, Michael.

"Get out of here, Mitchell. I never want to see you near Kat ever again," he ordered him.

Mitchell looked at him and the rest of them with disgust as he slithered away.

Kat walked over to her dad and commented, "Daddy, look at you with the right hook," giving him a high five.

"Are you okay, sweetheart?" he said, wrapping his arm around her.

Kat nodded. "I'll be okay. I was going to break it off with him anyway," she admitted to him.

"Kat, I should have told you he was here. I actually thought he left after I made him leave the Inn," Natalie told her.

"It's okay, Nat. He clearly was up to something."

Kat walked over to Jayson; whose lip was split open. "Are you okay?"

Jayson nodded. "Yeah. I just need to go home."

His eyes said it all. She had hurt him. She didn't mean to. She didn't mean for any of this to happen.

She watched as Jacob, Melissa, and Dennis took him home.

She was at a complete loss as to what she should do.

Chapter 41

Kat woke up the next day feeling as if she was hungover. Her body felt heavy. She was exhausted. Maybe it was due to everything that had happened the night before at the festival or the end of a very brief, but strained, engagement.

She should be happy that she was finally done with Mitchell, but seeing Jayson so defeated just made her even more confused.

This was the first night in the new house. Her queen-sized bed was beyond comfortable. The last thing she wanted to do was to get out and face the world. She looked around the spacious room that only had a new bed and a nightstand.

She had it painted cream with gray trim. The painters were slowly doing the other rooms one by one.

Groggily, she got up and walked over to her window and looked out at the bay. The sun reflected so beautifully off the water. She was still in disbelief that she owned the home that she always loved as a child.

As she walked back to the bed, her phone rang. She picked it up off of her nightstand. It was Thea.

"Morning," Kat answered in a groggy tone.

"Hi, I wanted to check on you. How are you doing?" Thea said with concern.

"I'm okay. I'm just pretty tired. What a night," Kat replied.

"That was so crazy. I can't believe Mitchell. I mean, what was that?"

Kat said, "I had no idea he did that to Jacques' mother, or Melissa or Nat. I mean, Nat. My sister. How could he? I really messed up when it came to him."

"Nah, there would have been no way that you would have known that he did that to Jacques Primeau's mother, Kat."

Kat shrugged as she sat on the foot of the bed.

"I'm floored Mitchell did the things he did. I wonder who else he's done that to?" Kat asked.

"Well, he's not your problem anymore. I wouldn't be surprised if he lost his real estate license," Thea said.

"Me either." Kat paused for a couple of seconds before she asked, "Hey, Thea, have you heard from Jayson?"

"I haven't. Jacob went home with him last night. He looks like he got a nice split lip though."

"God, I feel so awful. It's all my fault," Kat said.

"How? You didn't tell Mitchell to give Jayson a right hook," Thea replied.

"Of course not. But Jayson and I were getting a little close..."

"Oh?" Thea said with surprise.

"He doesn't want me to go back to the city," Kat told her.

"Well, how do you feel about that?" Thea asked.

"I am just getting my stride here at *The Post*. I love doing what I'm doing there. It's been fun getting to really know everyone and learning about all the different facets of what makes the paper work. I'll really miss it when I have to go back in a couple of weeks."

"I will miss you horribly. But you have that fabulous new farmhouse. You'll be coming home a lot."

"Yeah, there's so much room here. There's even room for a home office if I wanted to do some work from home," Kat told her.

"Well, if you have a laptop, phone, and Wi-Fi, do you really need to go back there to do your job?" Thea asked.

Kat thought about it. "Technically, no. But my stuff is there."

"There's an invention called movers. They have what's called moving trucks that can move your stuff anywhere you want," Thea teased her.

"This is true. It's something to seriously think about. I didn't realize how much I needed a reset. Don't get me wrong. I love what I do. I really do. But I really needed to be home."

"Well, I'll miss you," Thea said.

"I'll be home probably every weekend for a while. There are construction workers here every day. In fact, I better get dressed, the painters are painting the kitchen this afternoon so I'm going to grab some breakfast at The Hat Trick."

"I was about to go there myself. Maybe since prom season is over, I'll actually see my boyfriend," Thea said.

"Great, we'll have breakfast together. See you in a few," Kat said as they both hung up.

At The Hat Trick, Jacob was there helping out the staff with the breakfast rush. He had decided to stay at his parents' not only to touch base with his dad, but also make sure Jayson was okay.

He was concerned about his twin. Jacob knew the signs. The faraway looks, the constant concern, the protectiveness. Jayson still had feelings for Kat. It wasn't like they were when they were all kids, this was different. He saw it in Jayson's eyes when Kat couldn't answer. It shook him to his core. Jayson could fight and handle anything that came his way, but everything that happened the night before devastated him.

Jacob walked into his office and saw Jayson sitting there with an ice pack on his mouth. "Let me see?" Jacob said as he took the ice pack off. Jayson's lip was partially bruised and swollen. "You look beautiful," Jacob continued.

Jayson put the ice pack back on his lip. "Seriously, how are you feeling this morning? You were still asleep when I left."

Jayson looked perplexed. "I'll be okay. I don't know what the heck happened last night. He just came at me in such a rage."

Jacob rolled his eyes. "What a jerk. I'm still ticked off at what he did to Mom. Not once, but twice. I'm surprised she didn't deck him."

Jayson said, "I know, right? He would have deserved it, that's for sure."

Jacob sat on the edge of the desk. "Did you talk to Kat this morning?"

"No," Jayson replied. "She must be feeling such mixed emotions."

"I'm sure. She nearly married the creep. Not her fault."

"No, not at all," Jayson agreed.

"Better for her to know now, than later. He saved her a whole lot of heartache," Jacob said.

Jayson looked sad. "I don't want her to go, Jake."

Jacob paused for a second. He had a feeling this was going to happen. "Did you tell her?" he asked.

Jayson nodded. "I did. But she said she had to for now. "

"Didn't she get that huge farmhouse? If she's not staying, then why buy it?" Jacob asked.

"She'll be here a lot more, apparently. She's always wanted that house since we were kids. It was a dream of hers."

"Nice house. Well, give her some time. All of this has to be crazy for her," Jacob reminded him.

"I think we both need some space," Jayson told him.

Chapter 42

After meeting Thea for breakfast, Kat was both hopeful on one hand that she would see Jayson at the diner, but on the other hand, relieved when she didn't.

She didn't know what to say. She needed to apologize and just explain what she meant by what she said.

Everything that she felt about him was mixed, but there was a huge part of her that needed for him to understand. He had finally told the truth and maybe it was time for her to face some truths about herself.

Maybe I still want him in my life because I still love him? she wondered.

She drove to *The Post* and sat in the parking lot. *What would a relationship with Jayson look like now, after all these years?* she thought. They weren't teens, they both had demanding careers that took them all over the country. If he felt the same, how would this all work?

She put her head down on her steering wheel. A knock on her driver's side window had her look up to see Ross waving at her.

She put the window down.

"You look exhausted," he told her.

"I feel exhausted," she shared with him as she got out of the car.

"Then why are you here?" he asked her with a concerned look on his face. "No one expected you here today."

"The paper never sleeps, Ross. You taught me that," she reminded him as they both started walking into the building.

"How are you feeling?" he asked, putting his hand on her shoulder.

"Okay, I'll be okay. I was going to break up with Mitchell anyway." She smiled at him weakly.

"Your dad and grandmother should be here today to look at how the financials are going," Ross told her.

"I'm a nervous wreck about that too."

Ross stopped her dead in the hallway. "Why? Everything is going great. The paper is pretty much back on track. Your dad is feeling better. I doubt your grandmother is going to sell it now."

"I loved doing all of this, Ross. I loved helping and working here. I admire everyone's hard work and dedication here. I always said that putting a daily newspaper together is literally piecing together a puzzle. Each department is a piece. And every night by midnight, all of those pieces come together into a great edition. From advertising to editorial, this town has such a jewel in *The Post*."

"I loved working with you here. Not sure if I'm going to go back to New York, Kat," Ross admitted to her.

Kat looked confused. "What do you mean?"

"Well, I've been thinking about slowing down for a while. I'm not getting any younger and I have to say, I really like Sweetbriar. I love the bakery and the Inn and all of the little shops. The bookstore is marvelous," Ross told her.

Kat was saddened. She'd miss her boss. "Does anyone at the *Empire Post* know yet?"

Ross nodded. "I gave my notice this morning. Your friend, Candace, was nice enough to find a great place for me here in town."

"That's fantastic! Sounds like you've thought this through. Well, I'll still see you for a bit. I bought the Mulderry Farmhouse that's along the bay," she told him.

Ross' eyes lit up. "You did? When?" he asked.

"A couple of months ago. I closed on it about a week ago. It needs some work, but I'll be here a lot on weekends and holidays. The one thing I've learned from this too, is to slow things down," she admitted. "I was flying through so much that I didn't even pay attention to who was around me."

"There wouldn't have been any way for you to know he was doing that, Kat," Ross told her.

"Oh, I know. But there were things that he'd say and it would rub me the wrong way. Oh, well. He's gone now. He can be someone else's headache."

They began to walk again toward the newsroom when Ross asked, "Any word on Jayson?"

Kat nodded. "No, I was hoping to see him at the diner. But there's a part of me that was glad I didn't."

"Oh?"

"It's a little complicated. He and I have such a history. We started out as childhood friends, then childhood sweethearts, then enemies, then friends again, to now, I don't know what we are," she admitted.

"Take it a day at a time. You'll figure it out," he assured her as they made it to the newsroom. They were greeted by Mae and Michael in Michael's office.

"Hi, Daddy, and, Grandma," Kat greeted, giving them both a hug.

"Hello, sweetheart," Mae told her. Michael gave his daughter a kiss on the cheek. He also welcomed Ross by stretching out his hand.

"How ya doing, Ross? It was good talking to you last night," Michael said.

Ross smiled. "Same, I'm doing great. Thanks for the talk last night."

"Talk?" Kat said.

Michael explained, "Yeah, Ross and I had such a great talk about journalism and life. I'm so glad that you decided to stick around."

Ross said, "Me too. Glad to know that I got a couple of new friends in you and Dennis."

Michael snickered. "Yeah, Den is great. One of my best friends. Did you tell Kat about your new job?"

"No, I didn't," Ross said.

"New job?" Kat asked.

"You're looking at the new managing editor of *The Post*," he told her.

Kat smiled. "Ross, that's great! Congrats!" she said, giving him a hug.

"Kat, your father and I have been looking over the financials and I am impressed. There has been a fifty percent increase in revenue since you took over. All of the plans you and Ross have implemented are working. By year's end, the paper is on track to be back to normal," Mae said.

Kat was relieved. She was happy that her grandmother was pleased with her and the changes she had made.

"Thank you, Grandma. That means a lot. I didn't want you to sell *The Post*. It's our family's legacy. I have really learned to love having my hands in each and every department, I'll miss it. Dad is better now. His lifestyle is completely different now."

Michael looked at his daughter with pride.

"Kat, I'll be the first to tell you that I didn't think you could pull off all these changes. People love the online and mobile versions of the paper, the tie-ins with Jayson's column and podcast are working. Subscriptions are up, advertising is through the roof. I was so stuck in how we did things in the past that I was too scared to look forward. Which brings me to..."

"Kat, we know that you have a great career in New York. But we would like to offer you the job of editor and publisher of *The Sweetbriar Post*," Mae said.

Tears of happiness welled up in Kat's eyes. "I'd be honored, Grandma," she told her. Mae smiled. "But what about Daddy?"

Michael smiled widely. "Semi-retirement. I would love to write a column, but I realized that I need to slow down. I was stressed and I hated the business aspect of things around here. I am at heart a writer. You? You are the complete package. You're a writer, TV personality, and a badass boss. You have always been something special."

"You had to soar before you could return," Mae said.

Then it all clicked. Everything that Jayson had done, she understood it. It was all for this moment. It was as if he could predict what would happen.

Kat wiped the tears from her eyes. "Thank you both. I'll make you both proud," she told them. She turned to Ross and told him. "Guess who's moving back home?"

Ross laughed. "Congratulations, Katherine."

Chapter 43

KAT WENT BACK TO THE farmhouse. She was so happy to be staying here permanently. After her meeting with her grandmother and father, she and the *Empire Post* came to a deal where she would be a special guest contributor so that they wouldn't lose her permanently.

She could work remotely from Sweetbriar, while travelling, if she wanted to. She'd file stories for them either monthly or every other month.

The position not only freed her to work full time at *The Sweetbriar Post*, but also let her continue to interview the higher profile people she was known for.

Since she was free for rest of the afternoon, she figured she'd go home and begin arrangements to move and get her things.

She was looking at the work of the painters outside when a black truck pulled up. She didn't recognize the vehicle and figured it was lost.

She was about to walk up to it when Jayson got out of the truck.

She took a deep breath. She didn't know if she was ready to do this.

"Hello," she greeted him.

He had his sunglasses on and his upper lip was a little swollen.

"Hi. Did I catch you at a bad time?" he asked.

"No." She nodded. "How's your lip?"

"It'll be fine. I'm used to getting the shit knocked out of me," he admitted.

She walked over to him. "I am so sorry, Jayson," she said, her eyes filled with sadness.

"Not your fault, Kat. That guy is a jerk. "

"I should have said no to his proposal months ago. It didn't feel right from the start."

"You wanted to believe he was a good person. That's what I love about you," he told her. "You see the good in everyone."

"Couldn't see that. Jacques' mother, your mom, my little sister. I sure can pick them."

Jayson laughed. "Come on. Your beating yourself up for no reason. Was I that bad?" he asked.

"Once upon a time, yeah, you were. At least I thought you were. Now? You are an angel compared to him."

Jayson smiled. He took off his sunglasses and replied. "See?" he teased. He touched a stray curl that had went into her face.

She smirked. "I don't know what I'm going to do," she told him.

"About?" he asked.

"You. You are charming, hysterical, and I want to just—"

He brought her close to him. "And to just what?" he interrupted her. His hazel eyes looked at hers warmly.

"Let you back in," she admitted to him.

He leaned in and parted her warm lips with his. He had missed the sweet taste of her lips. "Why not?" he asked softly.

She pulled away from him. "I'm scared of what happened before, Jay."

"It won't happen again. I don't know what else to say, other than it won't. I was a scared kid who loved a girl so much that he let her go. Now, I'm a grown man who loves a woman so much that he doesn't want to let her go."

Her eyes were pleading with his. "In my head I believe everything you are saying. I want to try again. Whatever that is right now. But my heart is saying, wait," she told him as she grabbed his hand.

Jayson's eyes welled up. "I'll wait. However long it takes, I'll wait. I'm all in this time. I'd like for us to try this again. I won't mess up. I'll be the best guy you'll ever meet."

"You should know that I'm staying in Sweetbriar. My grandmother named me editor and publisher of *The Post*."

Jayson screamed for joy. "Yes! That's my girl! See what I'm talking about, Kit Kat?" His hands cradled her head. "You are so special. You needed to leave to come back even better. This is all I wanted for you."

"I just hate that you took my choice away," she told him.

"I shouldn't have. But let me ask you, if you had gone to Georgia State and maybe we had gotten married, what do you see yourself doing?" he asked

She responded, "I don't know. Maybe writing something, taking care of our child if we had one?"

"And would you have been dreaming of doing the stuff that you're doing now? If you hadn't left, your grandmother would have had to find and hire someone else to run the paper while your dad recuperated. Or who knows, she may have sold it. "

"Or maybe not," she said.

"She definitely would have had to hire someone to run things. Thanks to your experience, she didn't have to."

"I had help," Kat reminded him.

"So what? You knew what to do and you fixed it. Give yourself some credit."

"So, if we try this, what about your career?" she asked.

"What about it? I have a year left on my contract. It's not like I don't come home," he told her. "Look, my parents have had a long-distance relationship for years, and they love each other more now than they did when they were first married. We can do this."

She looked at him and smiled. "You make a convincing case," she teased. "Stop doing that."

"You know this can work. Let's just try it. One day, one step at a time," he urged her.

"Give me a little bit," she told him cautiously.

"Take as long as you need. I'm not going anywhere. I love you," he told her as he kissed her on the top of the head.

She looked at him as he got into his truck and drove off.

Maybe she was being too guarded. She knew he meant what he said in her mind, but her heart was stopping her. She just broke up with a jerk and maybe part of her was saying "slow down."

Maybe a little time was what was needed.

Chapter 44

JAYSON DROVE AROUND aimlessly. He didn't know where to stop or who to talk to. For the first time in a long time, he knew what he wanted. It was Kat. It had always been Kat. There was a familiarity, a comfort. What they had was special. She was the only one who could call him out on his crazy antics and face the person he saw in the mirror.

The more he tried to deny his lingering feelings for her, the harder he fell for her.

He wound up at his parents' house. It was a picturesque home next door to Kat's family's home. It was a typical white house with a huge wraparound porch.

He walked up the walkway and opened up the black door.

"Anyone home?" he shouted as he walked in.

Dennis came into the foyer from the kitchen. He was casually dressed in shorts and a T-shirt.

"Hey, son. What brings you here?" Dennis asked as he opened up a can of juice.

Jayson looked lost. "I was driving around and wound up here," he replied to him.

"Come on in," Dennis told him. "I'll grab you something? Juice, soda, sweet tea?"

"Nah, I'm good."

The two of them went into the family room and sat on the couch.

"I just came from seeing Kat," Jayson told his dad.

"How did that go?" Dennis asked as he took a sip of his juice.

"I guess you're right. I have unfinished business. I didn't know how much I missed her until the festival. I've been thinking about her nonstop since she got back. The more I try to fight it, the worse it gets."

Dennis smiled warmly. "I had a hunch you still had feelings for her. Does she know?" he asked.

Jayson leaned back on the couch. "She does. She's taken a job here at *The Post*. Mae made her editor and publisher of the paper."

"That's fantastic. Good for Kat. She's such a great person."

"She is."

"Well then, what's the problem?" Dennis asked.

"She wants time to think things through."

Dennis shrugged. "Well, she literally got out of an engagement last night. I understand that."

"Oh, I do too. I just don't know if I did the right thing by telling her," Jayson said.

"You totally did the right thing. If you hadn't, you would have regretted it."

"I was the one who broke it off the first time, now I want her back and she needs time."

"Then give it to her. Let her get settled in and then see how it goes."

"I told her that too. I told her about how you and Mom have made it work all these years having a long-distance relationship."

"And I love your mother more than I did back then," Dennis told him.

"I said that to her. I also kissed her."

Dennis' eyebrows raised. "Oh?"

"Uh huh."

"What happened after that?"

"She said her head is saying for her to trust me, and her heart is saying not yet."

"Well, you did put together an elaborate plan to break up with her. I get the trust issues," Dennis told him.

"It was so long ago. We're different people now. We're adults. We were kids back then. How I feel about her this time, feels so different. It's deeper. I don't know if I can deal if she says no."

"You'd be okay. You know, I remember when your mother and I were dating and there was this guy named Duke Watson, who lived in the next town over. He was so into your mother. But she didn't like him that way. They were friends forever. Even before we started dating. Your mother's favorite band, as you know, is Fleetwood Mac. And I tried to get us tickets one time when they were playing here at the amphitheater, but they had sold out. So Duke, in a quest to win your mother over, got Fleetwood Mac to play in the town square."

Jayson's eyes lit up with delight. "Shut up!"

"It was pretty impressive. Your mother was thrilled and literally in the middle of the concert, Duke proclaimed his love for her. I was ready to murder him. Your mother had told him time and time again that she didn't feel the same way about him. She was so mad that she pushed him away. Haven't seen Duke back in Sweetbriar since."

"Whoa."

"I'm telling you the story as a reminder to not push her. When and if Kat is ready, she'll let you know."

Jayson nodded. "Wonder what happened to Duke."

"I heard he's happily married and owns an auto body shop. So, despite his love for your mother, he got over it in time. Regardless of what happens, you'll be okay. It may not feel like it now, but it will be."

"I just want one more chance. One more."

"I hope you get it, son. I truly do," Dennis told him.

Chapter 45

A couple of days later, Thea went to see Kat at the farmhouse. Although she wasn't quite at the house yet, she could see—thanks to the long driveway—Kat was overseeing the workers putting up a new picket fence.

Like Kat, Thea had always loved this farmhouse. It was something out of a movie with its white exterior and full wraparound porch. As she rolled up the driveway, it reminded her of a soap opera she used to watch as a teen.

As she got out of her car. She heard Kat talking to the workers.

"When will it be done?" Kat asked.

"Oh, after we replace the broken poles, today. Then tomorrow we'll paint it and you'll be all set," the worker told her.

"Looks great," Thea said, walking up to the house.

"Hi, there," Kat greeted. "We're just finishing up the fence."

"I haven't seen or heard from you in a couple of days," Thea said.

"Oh, I'm fine. I've been busy making arrangements with getting my things transported. I have to grab my dog too," she told her.

"Grabbing your dog?" Thea asked.

Kat explained, "I'm adopting a shih tzu from the local shelter. They said I could pick her up in a couple of days. Also, my dad is going into semi-retirement, so my grandmother asked me to be the new editor and publisher of *The Post*."

Thea's eyes lit up. "So, does this mean that—"

Kat interrupted, "I'm staying!"

Thea squealed, "Yes!!!" She hugged her. "So glad my bestie is back for good! And you're getting a dog! Wait, what about your job at the *Empire Post*?"

"Well, we worked out a deal where I'll be a special contributor and I'll do a story either once a month or bi-monthly for them. That way, they won't lose me altogether. Management was apparently worried about circulation numbers if I left permanently. I can do that job anywhere. In fact, they're putting in the high-end cable and internet wiring tomorrow. "

"Have laptop will travel," Thea told her.

"I'll be doing some of that, but not for a while. I'll be busy with Ross, making sure *The Post* stays in the black. It's doing so much better. It's actually nice to take a few days off to clear my head and get things in order," Kat told her.

"Talk to Jayson?" Thea asked.

Kat took a deep breath as the two of them went onto the wraparound porch and sat on the steps.

"He came by a few days ago. He's doing okay. I apologized for putting him in that spot. I felt so bad that Mitchell did that to him because of me. He told me to not worry about it because he was used to being beaten up." Kat snickered.

Thea laughed. "He is. It's a daily occurrence during hockey season."

"Then he said what everyone else said about Mitchell. That it wasn't my fault. Mitchell was a jerk and I couldn't have known Mitchell would do that."

"See?" Thea told her.

Kat laughed. "I should just wear a tattoo on my forehead that says: Everyone told me so."

Thea laughed. "Love is blind, Kit Kat. You wanted to believe the best in him."

"That's what Jay said too. Said that's one of the things he loves about me," Kat said with a solemn look on her face.

"Oh?" Thea said.

"Yep. And he apologized for everything. Really apologized. I told him that I got the job offer at *The Post* and he just explained why he did what he did back then. Said if he could go back in time and change things, he would. He said he still loves me."

Thea smiled. "I had a feeling he did. How are you feeling about everything?"

"Honestly? I love him. I miss him. When he kissed me, it was if nothing had changed. But it has because we're older."

"Which is great because both of you have matured."

"All this time I felt like things were not done. He did too. Now, he wants us to try once more, despite him having to go back and play."

"Nothing wrong with a long-distance relationship. Dennis and Melissa have been doing it for years. I did it with Jake for a couple of years. It's a sacrifice but it's all worth it in the end," explained Thea.

"He said the same exact thing about his mom and dad. "

"Then what are you waiting for? Go with your heart," Thea told her.

"I want to. I really do. But something is just holding me back. What if he does what he did to me again?"

"Doubt it. He learned his lesson from that debacle."

"I don't know what I should do, Thea."

"I could sing Jayson's praises to death but you already know what a great guy he is. If he is telling you that he still has feelings for you, then he does."

"I know that. I know all of that. I know he's sincere. My head is like. Go Kat, tell him that you want to try again. But my heart is stopping things as if I am driving toward a roadblock."

"Maybe your heart is telling you that it's too soon after Mitchell. You were with him for a few years, Kat. Take some time, get your stuff from New York, get settled, and then see how you're feeling."

"Already doing it. I told him that I needed time."

"Listen, I'm selfish. I'm not only glad you'll be here all the time now, but I am praying that we get the Four Musketeers back together again. Especially now that we can all legally drink alcohol."

Kat laughed. "Of course. It's always about the alcohol."

"Always. We need a girls' night out. Since Shooter's is back open, we should get the girls together and go for a drink. Or two. Or three," Thea quipped.

"Actually, we should. We can celebrate me staying here, getting this house..."

"Getting back together with Jayson..." Thea said with a wink.

"Ha ha," Kat said.

"Seriously, whatever you decide, I'll support you," Thea told her.

Chapter 46

A few days later, Kat decided to get Candace, Thea, and her sister, Natalie, together for a girls' night out.

The three ladies met her at Shooter's after she left *The Post*.

"Hey!" Candace said as she, Thea, and Nat sat a table.

Kat smiled and sat down. "Hey, how are my girls?"

Natalie, who was already taking a sip of her screwdriver said, "It's been a day."

"Oh, no," Kat asked. "What happened?"

Natalie took a sip and replied, "Just the normal nonsense. We're short-staffed at the Inn so I'm running around for twelve hours a day like a chicken with its head cut off. And, my date the other night ghosted me."

"Are you serious?" Kat said. "Men are the worst." She shook her head in disbelief.

"Sure are." Candace chimed in. 'My husband insisted after I worked a twelve-hour day that his dinner should have been on the table at 6 p.m. He implied that since he owns two businesses in town, he was the primary breadwinner among us. I'm still heated about that two days later."

Thea's eyes narrowed. "What the heck? Does he realize that the prehistoric age ended years ago?"

"Right?" Kat said, her eyes were filled with bewilderment.

"Girl, you got lucky getting out of that relationship with Mitchell. You would have been dealing with the same BS," Candace said.

"I thought you guys were happy?" Kat asked with a look of confusion on her face.

Candace rolled her eyes and took a deep breath. "We are. I love him. But I don't know where that came from the other day. It literally came out of left field," Candace told them, taking a sip of her whiskey sour.

A waiter approached, "You ladies need anything?" he asked.

"I'll take a whiskey sour," Kat told him.

"I'll take another myself," Candace said.

"I'm good for now," Thea told him.

"Another screwdriver for me," Nat ordered.

"Coming right up," the young man said as he walked away.

"Enough about me for right now. How is everything going since you and Mitchell broke up?" Candace asked.

"Okay, I've been getting the farmhouse remodeled, my stuff is slowly getting shipped in from the city. I'm adopting a dog too. Oh, did I tell you that I'm moving back here permanently?" Kat told Candace.

Candace's eyes lit up. "Squee!!!" she said. "So great! I take it you're staying at *The Post*?"

"Gram made me editor and publisher of *The Post*. I think I'll be announced in this Sunday's edition. Dad's stepping down. He's going into semi-retirement. Guess he's digging not working so much. He'll be doing a column every so often."

"He looks great! I had to drop off some contracts for your mom to look at her office the other day and he was taking her to lunch. He looks like a new man," Candace said.

"He looks great. We're so grateful he's still with us," Natalie said. "That was such a close call."

"He said he'd never scare us like that again. I actually believe him. I think it scared him too," Kat told them as the waiter brought over their drinks and placed them down.

"Anyone check on Jay? Mitchell really clocked him. Telling you, after hearing everything he had done, I was ready to clock Mitchell myself," Candace announced.

"He's okay. He came by the farmhouse being his charming self. I felt bad for everything. Mitchell and I hadn't been getting along lately. I had been avoiding his calls and when we did talk, we were arguing. So, I think when Mitchell saw us dancing, he thought there was more going on than what there was."

Thea cleared her throat. "Ahem."

Kat looked over at her while she took a swig of her drink. "Spill it."

"Spill what?" Thea said feigning innocence.

"Just say what's on your mind because you know you want to," Kat said with a wink.

"Well, something did happen..." Thea smirked as she took a sip of her drink.

Nat and Candace gave them both a curious glance. "I was at my husband's booth so I didn't see what happened until that fight. What's Thea talking about?" Candace asked.

"Spill it, sis. We were giving out stuff for the Inn," Nat said with a smile.

Kat looked defeated. "Okay, Jayson begged me to stay in town that night. He told me he didn't want to lose me again. He realized he made a mistake years ago."

Candace was in shock. "Oh, finally! And what did you say?" she asked.

"That's the point, I really was in shock after that fight so I didn't know what to say. So, the next day, he comes to the farmhouse and we talk, and the next thing I know is we're kissing and he is begging for another chance."

Nat and Candace's eyes lit up with joy. "And what did you say?"

"I needed time," she told them. "I told him that part of me wants to, but I was scared that he'd pull another elaborate scheme when things got too serious. "

"But you realize he's older now and still loves you, right? I doubt he'd do that again. I think we wouldn't let him," Candace told her.

"I told her the same thing," Thea said.

"He wouldn't, Kat. We've known him forever. I had a feeling he still had a thing for you," Natalie shared with her.

"I think I just needed some space. I know he probably wouldn't. I guess, I'm just scared," Kat admitted.

"Well, it's normal and understandable. Now that you're getting settled, try it out. What's the worst that could happen?" Candace asked.

"World War III." Kat snickered as the three of them laughed and drank throughout the night.

Chapter 47

As Kat left to get into her car at Shooter's, Nicole ran out to stop her before she drove off.

"Hey, Kat, hang on!" Nicole yelled after her.

Kat turned around and stood in front of her car and asked, "What's up?"

Nicole took a few seconds to catch her breath. She replied, "Wanted to see how you were after everything that happened at the Harvest Festival."

"Aww, you're so sweet. I'm okay. Mitchell and I are definitely done, but I'm okay about things."

"What a jerk he was. Going after Jayson like that."

"I know. All we were doing was dancing and talking. It wasn't a big deal. Craziness," Kat said. "But I'm okay though."

"I'm glad. You deserve to be happy," Nicole told her.

"So do you. You should have joined us tonight."

Nicole laughed. "Aww, I was busy making sure things are up and running."

"I meant to tell you that the bar looks amazing. I had the best time here tonight. The band was great. The drinks, well... since I was driving, one drink, was great. You should be proud, Nicole."

Nicole smiled. "Well thanks, Kat. That means a lot coming from you. "

"I mean it. The bar is fantastic."

"I really want to say sorry about everything from a long time ago. I was so jealous of you and you were nothing but kind to me. I would have followed Jayson anywhere. He was gorgeous, kind, funny..."

"Oh, Nicole, it's okay. I know how manipulative he can be. It's fine. He and I talked about what happened and he explained his reasons why."

"What were they?" she asked.

"To live up to my potential. He didn't want to hold me back. He told me that if I had stayed and went to school here in Georgia, and if he and I had gotten married, I would have been resentful of him. He knew better than I did that there was more to my life than Sweetbriar back then," Kat explained.

"I remember us getting so drunk on the night that he wanted to go through with it and he kept saying that he loved you. After you left, he literally sat on the bed and he was crying. I tried to console him and I thought that I could take his pain away. It was then he said that he only loved you. He pushed me aside as if I were trash."

"I'm sorry, Nicole. You deserved better."

"Yeah, but I'll tell you this. At that Harvest Festival, the way he looked at you was the way he always used to look at you. I used to be in awe. He treated you back in school like a princess. You two were 'the' couple."

"We had problems like everyone else. But we did have fun back then. Before all of that, he was the perfect boyfriend for me back then. He listened to me, supported me, loved me. He was the best."

"I don't know, I think there's still a little something there. The way he looked at you the other night was the exact same way he looked at you when we were all in school," Nicole said.

"So you picked up on that too?" Kat said.

Nicole nodded. "Yes. That love doesn't happen every day. If you have it, grab it, hold on to it tight."

Kat smiled. "He is a good one. Despite him playing God." She snickered.

Nicole laughed. "Forgive him. I do. Everything he did was because he loved you. Don't throw it away because of something dumb," Nicole urged her.

Kat walked over to her and hugged her. Nicole smiled and tears welled up. She pulled away and said, "I was not expecting that."

"You put things into a perspective that I needed to hear. Thank you," Kat told her as she got into the car.

"Anytime. I promise you that next time, I'll join you for your girls' night."

"You better, you're one of us now. Give that cute son of yours a hug from me."

"I will. When's the next time you're in town?" Nicole asked.

"I'm moving here permanently. You're looking at the new editor and publisher of *The Sweetbriar Post*," Kat said turning on her ignition.

Nicole squealed, "Shut up! That's fantastic. Congrats!"

"I'll be having a housewarming party in a few days; I'd love for you to come. I bought the Mulderry Farmhouse."

Nicole smiled with glee. "I'd love to. Just let me know when."

"I will. I'll call you," Kat confirmed as she drove up the street and out of sight.

Nicole was so happy. All she wanted was to be included and to be forgiven.

But she realized that she needed to forgive herself. Now, she could begin the process of moving on completely from what happened years ago.

She was over Jayson. Even though his looks and Southern drawl still took her breath away, she knew now that he would always love Kat. There wasn't anyone else that could compete with that.

She hoped that one day, she would find someone. Someone who loved her as much as Jayson loved Kat. She wanted that so much for her and her son. Everything else was perfect. She had a great business, she was in a good place with her siblings and grandmother, and her son gave her such joy.

Whatever life had in store for her, she was ready to take it on.

Chapter 48

Jayson sat at the orthopedist's office in Atlanta. It was his monthly check-in on his knee. He brought Jacob as his support system.

The two of them sat in the examination room while the doctor came in.

"Thanks for coming with me," Jayson said to his twin.

"Of course. How's it feeling?" Jacob asked, as he pointed to his brother's knee.

"It feels pretty good. Hopefully, I'll get the okay to start working out on the ice so that I can get back to work."

Jacob looked at his brother with concern. "You don't want to push that. I tried and that ended my career. Let it heal on its own."

Jayson touched his knee. "I'm not. I'm just ready to get back."

"And away from Kat?" Jacob asked.

Jayson dismissed his brother's remark. "No, I miss my team. I miss playing. It has nothing to do with her. All this sitting around, going to physical therapy and exercising is making my anxiety go through the roof."

"But you haven't been just sitting around. You've been helping me at the diner and going to *The Post*," Jacob retorted.

"I sit at *The Post* writing. I sit for hours there."

"While watching her in her office," Jacob teased with a wink.

Jayson sighed. "Okay, maybe that's a problem. I can see if Mort will move my cubicle. But, to be honest, it'll be great today to get an all clear so I can start working out on the ice. The quicker I get back in shape, the quicker I can go back."

"And the less you have to deal with her," Jacob told her.

Jayson gave him an annoying glare.

"Jay, she asked for time. I don't see what the big deal is."

"It's not. If I leave, she won't be reminded of how things are every single time she sees me. I'm trying to give that to her."

"But rushing isn't going to help your knee if you reinjure it and can't play. Then what are you going to do?" Jacob asked him.

"You sound like Mom right now."

"Good, because someone should. Just take it easy. For years, you told us that you have been going full throttle. Between practice and playing and working out and then appearances. Let's not forget filming commercials or photo shoots for your endorsements on your days off. I am, for one, happy to see you home and doing hardly anything."

"What if, after giving her time, she turns me down?" Jayson asked with concern.

Jacob shrugged. "Then you will move on, Jay. It'll hurt. But you'll be okay."

"I'm going to be honest. It's always been her. Since we were kids. The first girl I had a crush on, my first real girlfriend. Regardless of who I've dated since, it always goes back to her."

"Does she know this?" Jacob asked.

"Yes. But she doesn't trust me, which I completely understand."

"I really don't think it has to do with that whole thing. I think it was everything that had to do with Mitchell and coming back and all that happened with her father. Now that she's staying and getting settled, try talking to her again," Jacob instructed

Jayson groaned.

"She's having a housewarming party at the farmhouse in a couple of days. Come with me and Thea."

"Oh, she sent me a text on that," Jayson told him as he held up the phone with Kat's text message.

Jacob's eyes lit up. "See, then it's not over if she did that. Come with us and have fun. What's the worst that could happen?"

"I say something wrong and get food on me?" Jayson teased.

Jacob let out a huge belly laugh. "I have to admit that was so funny when she did that. Not once, but twice. And then Thea?"

Jayson gave him a blank stare as his brother continued, "I think those days are over. I'm selfish. I miss all four of us hanging out together at the bay with a huge bonfire, talking about nothing. Regardless of what her answer is, she'll always be your friend."

Jayson nodded. "That's what I'm afraid of."

"Is that really a bad thing?" Jacob asked.

"No," Jayson replied.

"Then, come with us to the housewarming party. Have a couple of drinks, some awesome Southern food ,because you know she and Mae can throw down in the kitchen, and talk to her."

Jayson looked at him with reluctance and said, "Okay, I'll go. But if I get food or any kind of drink on me. It's on you."

"I doubt it'll happen. So, I'm all in on us having a great time and getting the band together once and for all," Jacob said as the doctor opened the door.

"Hello, gentleman," a female voice said. "How are we doing today?"

"We're good, Doc," Jayson told her.

The doctor was pretty with red hair and blue eyes, she appeared to be in her early forties. "Good to hear!" she said jovially. "Let's take a look at your knee," she told him as she pulled up his pants leg. "How's it feeling?"

"It feels pretty good. Sometimes, it hurts if I've been on it for a long time. But other than that, it's good," Jayson told her.

She looked at the long vertical incision and examined around his knee.

"It's healing nicely. The incision looks good," she remarked.

"So, I can start working out on the ice?" he asked eagerly.

She nodded. "I think you can. It actually looks and feels great. We'll take some pictures to be sure and I'd like you to take it slow. You have a few months to go before you really can get back. Once we have the MRI photos, you should be good to go."

Jayson was relieved. "Yes! Thank you, Doc."

Jacob smiled. "Thank you, Doc, he's been driving us all crazy."

The doctor laughed. "I bet. I'll be right back and we'll have the nurse take you down to the MRI room," she told him as she left.

Jayson smiled with glee. "Woo! Thank you, God! Let's go!" he said, touching his knee.

Jacob teased, "One happy ending down, one more to go."

Chapter 49

Jacob and Thea took his car to Kat's housewarming party. Thea was dressed in one of her designs. A black strapless dress with a blue shawl on her lap. Jake was dressed in a pair of black pants and a blue shirt.

"Do we really have to dress up for this?" Jacob asked.

"Yes, she said cocktail dress appropriate," Thea told him. "I guess some high-end magazines and other VIPs will be there. She'll be having a regular pool/bay informal day for the four of us tomorrow."

"The four of us?" Jacob said. "Does this mean what I think it means?" He turned to her with surprise.

Thea shrugged. "I have no idea. Let's look at the road, babe. I'd like to get to my best friend's home in one piece," she told him.

Jacob turned his gaze back on the road.

"Is Jay coming?" Thea asked

"Yeah, he was going to come with us. But he had some things to finish up at *The Post*, so he'll meet us there," Jacob told her.

"How was his MRI?" Thea asked.

"He got the all clear. He's ready to start working out."

"Well, that's great. I know he must miss his team."

"I think he's using this now as an excuse to get out of town," Jacob told her.

Thea looked at him with confusion. "Why does he want to leave?"

"He wants to give Kat some space. So, to do it, he figures that if he gets the all clear he can go back to the city and work out. Thus avoiding her."

Thea rolled her eyes. "Are you serious? What is wrong with him? First, he does this scheme, then he doesn't tell her that it was a plan, now he admits he has feelings for her and he wants to run? It's not like we don't have an indoor rink here? He can work out here in town until it's time to go back."

"That made my head spin," Jacob commented.

"We have to stop this," Thea said.

"How? If Kat wants to be with him, she'll let him know."

"Of course. But we just have to get them in a room together. This has got to stop. Honestly, I love your brother, but he gives me anxiety," Thea told Jake.

"Well, you better get used to that if we go down the aisle. When we love, we love hard."

Thea touched his leg. "That you do."

"What do you think she'll do?" Jacob said.

"I honestly don't know. Whatever she decides, she at least seems open to having him as a friend," Thea told him.

"I told him that he shouldn't worry about a food war. Hopefully, he doesn't listen to me and either wears something with Scotchgard or brings a change of clothes," Jacob quipped.

Thea laughed.

They pull into the long driveway. A man dressed in black and white came out of the home and greeted them as they got out.

"I'll take your car, sir?" the young man told Jacob as he helped Thea get out of the car.

"Take it where?" Jacob asked.

"To park it, sir. I'm the valet for the evening," he told them.

Jacob pursed his lips. "Good Lord. Okay, not a scratch on her. She's new," he instructed the young man.

Thea snickered. She leaned in and whispered to him, "Be nice."

"I'm always nice, Thea. Until you mess with my car or my girl," he told her as he pressed his lips on her forehead. "You look beautiful, by the way."

"Thank you. You look handsome."

"See, I clean up nicely when I want to."

"You really do," she told him as they walked into the refurbished home.

The house looked like something out of *Architectural Digest*. The old farmhouse still had its old Southern charm, but with a modern feel. Everything was freshly painted and with the latest technical upgrades. The home was mainly painted in different tones of gray, beige, and off white. The foyer was spacious. There were a ton of people walking around and admiring the photos of Kat through various stages of her life and career. From the photos of the Four Musketeers to photos with the Duchess of Sussex, Kat had been living a life that most people in Sweetbriar only dreamed of.

As Thea and Jacob looked at the photos of the Four Musketeers, Kat tapped them both on the shoulders.

She looked beautiful wearing a navy blue dress with spaghetti straps. Her hair was down and framed her face.

"Welcome to my humble abode," she greeted them both.

Thea hugged her. "You look beautiful," she told her friend.

"It's a Thea Morales original. I only wear the best," Kat told her.

Jacob hugged her. "You look fantastic. How are you doing?"

"I'm great. I'm feeling pretty good. Think I'm finally settling in."

"Well that's good," he told her.

"Yeah. I know that dressing up isn't really your thing. But the *Empire Post* wanted to showcase my new digs in their Lifestyle section, so there are a bunch of VIP's from Atlanta and New York here. Tomorrow is our day," she informed them.

Jacob looked around. "This house is beautiful. It's even nicer than I remember," he told her.

"It really is. You did a great job, Kat," Thea complimented her.

"Well, there's a few more little things. But the bulk of it is done," she told them.

"Thanks for coming by the way. Did you guys want anything? Wine? Beer? There are servers walking around with food. So help yourself," she told them as she continued to mingle with the others from the town and business people that they didn't know.

Thea noticed that Kat was looking around nervously. She turned to Jacob and said, "I think she's looking for him."

Jacob grabbed some shrimp off of a server's plate as he walked by and popped it in his mouth.

"Who?" he asked, as he was concentrated more on his food than what Kat was doing.

"I think she's wondering where Jay is," Thea said.

Jacob looked at his watch and shrugged. "Well, I am too. He was supposed to be here by now."

Thea looked over at Kat. She looked around and her face filled with sadness as the night went on. There was no sign of Jayson.

Later on as the two of them continued to mingle with other townspeople, Kat came over to them. "Okay, do either one of you know where Jayson is?" she asked, her voice filled with desperation.

Jacob looked upset. "I thought he'd be here by now. He must have gotten held up at the paper."

Kat's smiled turned into sadness. "I guess so. Well, there was something I wanted to tell him. But I guess, it'll have to wait."

Jacob and Thea nodded. Jacob looked at his watch. "It's getting late. We better go. We'll see you tomorrow?" he confirmed with Kat.

Kat nodded.

"He'll be here tomorrow, honey. I'm sure he just got held up," Thea told her as she gave her a hug.

"Thanks again for coming. I'll see you both tomorrow," Kat reminded them.

Kat's eyes filled with frustration as the two left. She had hoped Jayson would be here. She had to let him know how she felt.

Chapter 50

K at walked around her house and began to pick up some things that were left over from her housewarming party.

By all accounts, it was a success. The VIPs and colleagues of the *Empire Post* were all happy. The townspeople and friends seemed to like everything. But there was something missing.

Where was he? she wondered. *It would have been great to have him here.*

She continued to go from room to room, picking up empty plates and glasses. She'd have the cleaning service clean the house in the morning.

She took off her heels and began to lock up the front when there was a knock at the door.

She opened it. And there he was. He looked dapper in a pair of black pants and a gray shirt. He appeared to be awkward and nervous.

"Hi," she said with a disappointed tone.

"Hey, I'm sorry. I got caught up with my column. Mort needed some changes and they took a while. Am I too late?" he asked.

Even though she was disappointed, she smiled weakly at the effort. "Yes, but it's fine. You're here now," she told him.

"Can I come in?" he asked.

She opened the door wider and let him in.

He looked around the foyer as she trailed behind. "This looks great, Kit Kat," he praised.

"Thanks, it's nearly all done. Just have a couple of minor things left to do. I wanted to get the bulk of it done before the rest of my things got here."

"Nice," he responded to her as he looked at the wall of photos across from him.

"So many photos, so many memories," she said him.

"I still can't believe you met the Duchess of Sussex," he snickered.

Kat smiled. "She's really sweet. I actually still talk with her every now and then. You'd be surprised how down-to-earth she is."

"I believe it. I get it all the time. Only difference with our jobs is that we have a camera on us twenty-four seven."

"Or a journalist wanting to know what your favorite dessert is or who you're dating," she teased.

He leaned over to her. "That would be strawberry pie and as for dating? Hopefully, you," he whispered.

Kat chuckled. "So, it's still the pie. I guess some things never change." Her hand touched his arm.

"So are we going to finally talk about this or are we done?" he turned to her and asked. "Because, babe, if this is it. I have to go. I love you. I can't stay here, it's too much," he confessed with tears in his eyes.

"I love you too," she told him as she grabbed his hand. "I was hoping that you'd be here tonight. I needed you. You would think that I would be used to all these people around, but the truth is I'm not. You were and always have been my rock. Even if you drove me crazy."

He laughed.

"We have a bit of work to do, but if you want to do this, I'm all in," she told him.

He cupped his hands around her face and kissed her gently on the lips. Her legs nearly buckled from the feelings she had for him. He briefly pulled away.

"Thank God that's over," he joked.

Kat laughed as he continued, "I will spend my life making up for all the lost time we missed. I have a year to go on my contract but we can make it work."

"We'll make it work. Promise me, no more crazy schemes. If you have an issue, let's talk about it."

He kissed her on the forehead. "I promise. No more schemes. Unless you're in on it," he quipped.

"That's my guy," she told him as they walked through the house holding hands.

"By the way, I got the all clear to start working out so I'll be back on the ice sooner than later," he informed her.

She smiled widely. "Yes!! You mean, I can now come to your games and be your cheerleader?" she asked.

He picked her up. "You better!"

"Whoo hoo!" she screamed as he spun her around. He put her down.

She leaned against him. Her head laid softly against his chest. She had forgotten how safe she felt when she was in his arms. It was a feeling that she never really had with Mitchell. She never thought she would have this feeling again. She closed her eyes and listened to his heart beat. His strong hands caressed the small of her back as she moved in closer to him.

"I could do this all night," he whispered, his breath was warm against her skin.

She moaned with satisfaction. "Then, let's do that," she told him as she walked him toward the bedroom.

"Are you sure?" he asked her.

"Never more sure of anything in my life," she assured him.

"Wait 'til Jake and Thea hear that we're back," he told her.

"Well, they'll be here tomorrow afternoon. So they'll see it. It'll just be the four of us. Just like old times."

"Yes, but first..." Jayson said as he picked Kat up, and gave her a kiss. "We have some unfinished business."

The two of them went into the room and shut the door. For the first time in a long time, both of them were all in.

The End